"That's Quite a Horse You've Got There, Mister,"

the stranger said with a sardonic grin. "I think I'll just take him off your hands. Unbuckle your guns while you're at it."

Lassiter studied the young man, noting his continuous nervous gestures and the way he would occasionally glance around, fearing that someone might come along. His mule carried more supplies than any one man would need.

"You wouldn't leave me out here afoot, would you?" Lassiter asked him, stalling for time.

"Fort Benton ain't that far," the thief replied. "Where you from, anyway?"

"I just rode up from Colorado," Lassiter told him. "I heard folks up here were friendly. I guess I heard wrong," Lassiter said, easing his hands down to his gunbelt.

"Careful," the man warned, leaning forward with his pistol. His impatience was growing. "Hurry up with them guns."

Lassiter turned his head and looked beyond the young man. "Who are those two men?"

The thief instinctively reacted and turned to look. He realized his mistake too late and turned back, firing wildly . . .

Books by Loren Zane Grey

Published by POCKET BOOKS

Most Pocket Books are available at special quantity discounts for bulk purchases for sales promotions, premiums or fund raising. Special books or book excerpts can also be created to fit specific needs.

For details write the office of the Vice President of Special Markets, Pocket Books, 1230 Avenue of the Americas, New York, New York 10020.

LOREN ZANE GREY

LASSITER'S SHOWDOWN

POCKET BOOKS

New York   London   Toronto   Sydney   Tokyo   Singapore

An *Original* Publication of POCKET BOOKS

 POCKET BOOKS, a division of Simon & Schuster Inc.
1230 Avenue of the Americas, New York, NY 10020

ISBN: 0-671-70165-7

First Pocket Books printing May 1990

10 9 8 7 6 5 4 3 2 1

POCKET and colophon are registered trademarks of
Simon & Schuster Inc.

Printed in the U.S.A.

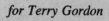

for Terry Gordon

LASSITER'S
SHOWDOWN

1

THE UPPER MISSOURI RIVER in late June ran cool with mountain snowmelt though the midafternoon sun was less than comforting. Lassiter's long ride north into Montana Territory had brought him this far, just short of Fort Benton. He decided to take a rest in the shade of the cottonwoods along the river.

Lassiter and his stallion refreshed themselves from a small spring that seeped up from gravels among the trees. After a long drink and a splash of cold water against his face, Lassiter turned to see a rider sitting his horse a short ways behind him. The man had a rifle leveled at him.

"That's quite a horse you've got there, mister," the rider said with a sardonic grin. "I think I'll just take him off your hands."

The rider was young, and he had a wild look in his eyes. His hat and clothes were saturated with dust. He led a large gray mule laden with flour and coffee, more supplies than any one man needed. Lassiter considered the possibility that more thieves could be nearby.

"Unbuckle your guns while you're at it," the thief added, eyeing Lassiter's twin, black-handled Colt .44s. "I kind of like them, too."

"Tell you what, kid," Lassiter suggested, easing away from his stallion, "you leave me your horse and that mule with all the supplies, and I'll let you have my stallion. Fair trade?"

The thief looked puzzled. Then he laughed. "Who you trying to kid?" he asked nervously. "This ain't no trading deal, here. I want your horse and your guns, both. You ain't getting nothing from me."

Lassiter studied the kid, noting his continuous nervous gestures and the way he would occasionally glance around, fearing that someone might come along.

"You wouldn't leave me out here afoot, would you?" Lassiter asked him, stalling for time.

"Fort Benton ain't that far," the thief replied. "Where you from, anyway?"

"I just rode up from Colorado," Lassiter told him, looking for an edge of some kind.

"A long ways from home, ain't you?" the thief said with a grin. Then he turned serious. "I said undo them guns, right now!"

"Take it easy," Lassiter said, easing his hands down to his gunbelt.

"Careful," the kid warned, leaning forward with his rifle. "Be real careful."

"I heard folks up here were friendly," Lassiter told him. "I guess I heard wrong."

"It don't matter what you heard," the young thief said angrily. His impatience was growing. "Hurry up with them guns."

Lassiter turned his head and looked beyond the kid. "Who are those two men?"

The thief instinctively reacted and turned to look. He realized his mistake too late, and turned back, firing wildly at Lassiter, who had already stepped sideways with one large Colt cleared. Lassiter fanned his revolver, riddling the thief with bullets.

Lassiter watched the kid's wild eyes widen even more as he yelled and clutched at his chest. He toppled sideways and out of the saddle, as his black mare sidestepped away from the pallid smoke curling from Lassiter's Colt.

A common thief too sure of himself, Lassiter thought while he wondered if there were others nearby. Lassiter took cover momentarily to be certain the gunfire didn't bring any of his friends.

Nothing but flies showed up, and Lassiter concluded the thief must have been on his own. It was possible he had been sent into Fort Benton for supplies by others in a gang. If that was the case, he should have stuck to his original chore.

Lassiter led the black mare over and tied the dead thief over the saddle. After he gave her a good swat on the rump, the mare broke into a gallop. She would eventually find her way back home.

Lassiter led the mule to his red stallion and mounted. The supplies would likely come in handy. His journey to Fort Benton was at the request of a good friend, who had wired him from Helena a week earlier with an urgent message. Lassiter had been given a note at the hotel in Helena asking him to travel on to Fort Benton, as quickly as possible.

Knowing Ben Morris, with whom he had trailed long-horns up from Texas a few years before, Lassiter was certain he would be headed where coffee and flour were hard to come by. Anytime he had traveled with Morris, they had been far away from civilization.

Lassiter gave the message more thought on his way into Fort Benton and concluded Ben Morris had gotten himself into some serious trouble. Morris could hold his own with any man and wasn't one to take unreasonable chances. Lassiter continued to think about Morris's situation as he rode down Fort Benton's main street. The town was a beehive, filled with cowhands and traders, miners and rivermen, gamblers and wagon-seat salesmen. Laughter and saloon music blared from rows of saloons and dancehalls. Grand hotels accommodated wealthy patrons, while the back alleys were lined with rows of log cribs and tents.

A steady flow of people scrambled back and forth from the levee along the river, where two steamboats were docked. Fort Benton was the main shipping point in the North, the end of the line for steamboat traffic up from St. Louis and points beyond. Bullwhackers and mule skinners freighted supplies south to the gold fields, and into the burgeoning cow country to the north and east.

Lassiter tied his stallion and the mule in front of Marshall and Gray's Saloon. Inside, the bar was clogged, and Lassiter shouldered his way through. A few noticed his twin Colts and black attire; he never went anywhere that he didn't draw some attention.

Among those who noticed him was Ben Morris, who stood up from a table in a far corner and joined him at the bar.

After shaking Lassiter's hand and slipping the cork from a bottle of rye whiskey, Morris began talking about old times and the cattle drive up from Texas.

"I don't think any of those cowhands have ever seen a man use a gun like you did, before or since," he commented, downing a drink quickly. He poured another. "How've you been keeping yourself?"

Lassiter sipped from his own glass and studied his old

friend. "I've been doing real well, thank you," he told Morris with a nod. "How about you?"

"I've been here and there," Morris said. "Haven't pushed any more cattle, though. I understand this country is starting to look for herds, though. I might see what I can scare up here."

"That's not why you wanted me to come all the way up here, is it, Ben?" Lassiter asked.

Morris shook his head. "No, of course not. I'm working on getting around to telling you about it. I just don't know how you'll take it."

"Try me," Lassiter said.

"Let's go back to that far table," Morris suggested. "I want you to be comfortable." He picked up the bottle and replaced the cork.

Lassiter followed Morris over to the table and waited for his friend to open up. Averting his eyes, Morris poured Lassiter another drink.

"You ever hear of amnesia?" he finally asked.

Lassiter nodded. "What's the matter? Did you forget something?"

Morris ignored the humor. "I'm serious. I have to find a woman who has amnesia. I need you to help me." Morris pulled from his pocket a small portrait of an attractive woman standing beside her husband, who was dressed nicely and seated in a large chair. He was a number of years older than she.

"She should stand out in a crowd," Lassiter observed.

"Her name is Lorna Jackson," Morris explained. "That's her husband, Darren. He used to look after me as a kid while my ma taught school. I told him that as a favor I'd go and find her for him, being he's a judge in Kansas City and can't get away. I didn't know at the time that she was headed all the way up here. I don't know what she'll say, once I talk to her.''

''You had me come all the way up here to help you find somebody who won't even realize she's been found?'' Lassiter asked. ''Why couldn't you do that on your own?''

''There's a hell of a lot more to it than that,'' Morris replied. ''This woman doesn't know where she is half the time, and she's headed into dangerous country. I can't help her alone. I've got to have you help me. Darren said he'll pay you; he just wants his wife back.''

''What brought her up here?''

''That's where the amnesia comes in,'' Morris began. ''She took a fall from a horse almost a year ago and banged her head. Ever since, she's been talking about locating a lost sister. She never even mentioned she had one until the horse accident. After that, she kept taking off on her own. People would bring her back, confused and crying. She didn't remember who she was or why she'd left.''

''Can't a doctor help her?'' Lassiter asked.

''It doesn't seem so. She keeps disappearing. This time Darren's really worried.''

''Are you certain she even has a sister?'' Lassiter asked.

''Lorna came out on the Oregon Trail when she was just four years old,'' Morris told Lassiter. ''She never did know her parents, and she grew up in a foster home. They told her after she'd grown up that she had an identical twin sister who had drowned in the North Platte River on the way West. At least, they thought she'd drowned. She'd wandered off from camp, and no one ever saw her again.''

''Now she thinks the sister isn't dead?'' Lassiter asked.

Morris nodded. ''After the fall from the horse, she talked about the sister a lot. Then something happened, according to Darren, that convinced her she was right about her sister being alive. One day an older woman came into Darren's office while Lorna was there and stared at her. She accused Lorna of being with a gang of outlaws who had held up a bank in Helena a few years before. The woman had been there at the time, and she swore Lorna was an outlaw. The next day, Lorna disappeared.''

"You certainly seem convinced this twin sister is alive."

"I've come to that conclusion," Morris explained. "At first, people would tell me they had seen Lorna, a pretty woman in a blue dress. When I got up here, a couple of people who looked at the picture told me I was trailing an outlaw."

Lassiter shook his head. "How long have you been following her?"

"Two weeks. It wasn't hard to find people who had seen her. She does stand out in a crowd. I know right where she's headed. She left with a mule skinner for a little town called Rocky Point, way the hell and gone in the badlands east of here. The way the hands in this saloon talk, you'd better write a letter home before you go out into that country. You might not make it back."

Lassiter looked around the room, noting the clientele. If the men he saw drinking and yelling were afraid of the badlands, there had to be a good reason.

"What makes Rocky Point such a poor choice for visiting?" Lassiter asked Morris.

"A gunfighter named Carson Hays and his two brothers operate near there," Morris replied. "The Hays boys and their gang of thieves hole up in a hideout somewhere in the badlands around there. They'll do about anything for a fast dollar or two. Mostly steal horses."

"And you're afraid this woman you're looking for is going to run into them somehow?" Lassiter wanted to know.

"I don't think there's any doubt about it," Morris said with a nod. "I showed Lorna's picture to an old miner who was drinking in here a few days ago. He was one of those who told me I had my hands full. I bought him a few drinks and got him to tell me about this outlaw queen. Her name is Lanna Hays. She used to be, or still is, married to Carson Hays, but she's on the run from him."

"Lorna Jackson's identical twin sister?" Lassiter asked.

Morris nodded. "Now do you see the complications?"

"How are you going to stop her before she runs into these outlaws?" Lassiter asked.

"That's why I sent for you," Morris said.

"I may have already met one of the gang myself, just outside of town," Lassiter then informed Morris. "He tried to steal my stallion."

"I doubt that he's alive then," Morris concluded.

"No, he's not alive, and I have a big mule loaded with supplies that he had with him."

"That will save us a trip to the general store," Morris commented. "Shall we be on our way?"

Lassiter followed Morris out into the street. To the surprise of both men, the gray mule was gone. Lassiter looked around as he unhitched his horse and climbed on.

"There must have been some other thieves with that kid," he said. "We're going to have to keep close watch now all the way."

2

BEN MORRIS climbed on his horse, and his eyes widened. Three men were rushing from the alley between the saloon and a general store next door. Morris yelled to warn Lassiter as the gunmen opened fire. He fell from the saddle, groaning, as his horse reared and ran down the street.

Lassiter felt the sting of a bullet crease his arm and another his leg as he swung down from his red stallion and pulled his twin Colts. The four gunmen became bolder and ran out from alongside the building.

From behind a water trough, Lassiter shot the first man who came into view, sending him reeling backward over a hitching post. Two frightened horses snapped their reins loose and bolted down the street.

Another gunman charged Lassiter's position, fanning his pistol. Lassiter ducked bullets that riddled the top and sides of the water trough. The gunman cursed when the hammer finally slammed the firing pin into dead shells.

Lassiter rose and drove the outlaw down into the street

with a series of blasts from his twin Colts. The third gunman burst down the alley in the other direction, and Lassiter fired a quick shot. The outlaw was hit but scrambled to his feet and began to run, holding his left arm as he disappeared behind a building.

Lassiter's first impulse was to chase the last gunman down, but he remembered Ben Morris, who was trying to raise himself up from the dusty street.

"Just lie still," Lassiter said. "There's a doctor coming." He knelt down next to his friend. Morris held his arm stiff from a hole just below the left elbow, and blood seeped from a lower right leg wound. Neither appeared too serious.

"I'll live," Morris told Lassiter through clenched teeth. "Don't let that last one get away."

Lassiter spotted the third gunman emerging from an alley four buildings down. He ran, both Colts drawn, as the gunman tried to mount his horse with his one good arm. The horse bolted out from under him, and he fell on his back into the street.

With one of Lassiter's Colts aimed at his head, the gunman coughed painfully and rose slowly to his feet. His left arm was crooked where the bullet had shattered it at the elbow. He was young and skinny, with a good week's growth of stubble on his face. He stood glaring at Lassiter while a number of men arrived and surrounded him.

"This young fellow here just tried to kill me and my friend," Lassiter told the men.

None of the men had ever seen the young kid before, and Lassiter asked him if he knew anything about a big gray mule laden with supplies.

"Nothing," the kid said.

"I'll bet if I look in the alley, I'll find him," Lassiter told the kid.

"You'll get yours, mister, I'll promise you that," the kid slurred. "I work for Carson Hays. You already killed three of his men. You don't push yourself up against Carson Hays and live to tell about it."

Lassiter remembered Hays's name. Now his gang was short four members.

"Your thieving days are over," Lassiter told the kid. "Maybe you'll be around to see this Hays fellow looking out from behind the same bars as you."

"Or maybe you'll be looking up from a grave," the outlaw suggested.

"Not likely," Lassiter said with a slight smile. He'd heard it all before, and from better men than the scraggly young outlaw in front of him. "You'd better worry about the shape you're in."

"The marshal's out serving a warrant," one of the men said. "But there's a deputy here who'll hold him behind bars."

"I ain't going to no jail," the young outlaw stated emphatically.

"Maybe you'd rather hang," another one of the men suggested. "We'd just as soon hang a horse thief as put up with any back talk."

"You'd better behave yourself and go to jail without a fuss," Lassiter suggested. "Carson Hays isn't here to back you up now."

The young outlaw realized he had no chance of escape and if he wanted to stay healthy, he'd better go to jail. Two men came forward, and the outlaw reluctantly allowed them to bind his hands tightly behind him with a rope. He bit his lip clear through trying not to yell out from the pain.

"We'd better have the doc look at his arm," one of the men recommended.

"After he gets through with my friend," Lassiter said.

Lassiter walked back to where a doctor was tending to Ben Morris. Neither wound would result in any serious complications; there was no bone damage, and none of the major blood vessels had been punctured. Morris was going to have to take it easy for a time, however; the doctor told Lassiter not to expect his friend to be able to ride for two or three weeks at the earliest.

"Here we go again," Morris said with a laugh. "Seems like something similar happened on the trail up from Texas."

"That was worse," Lassiter told Morris.

"It's going to keep me from going with you, though," Morris said. "Will you go ahead without me, Lassiter?"

"I'll have to," he answered. "That woman is likely almost to Rocky Point by now."

"I've got to be careful where I meet you from now on," Morris told Lassiter. "Every time I'm near you and a saloon, the fireworks begin."

Lassiter wanted to laugh with Morris, but his mind was on other matters. He was all alone, looking for a woman who didn't even know her own name. He knew the trouble was just beginning.

It was sundown when Carson Hays led eight men and twenty stolen horses into their hideout, deep in the badlands. The hideout was two abandoned wolfers' cabins in a large draw north of the Missouri River. The cabins had been built against the side of a high cliff where the bottom widened out into a grassy park. The country all around was steep and difficult to negotiate. Anyone coming in would have to know right where he was going.

As Hays and the others negotiated a steep trail down into the bottom, he could see his brothers, Lonnie and Jeff, coming out of the main cabin to greet him. They were soon joined by the rest of the gang, all of them watching and talking with approval about Carson's good catch of horses.

But Carson Hays wasn't eager to hear the men praise his fortunes. He was the one who dealt out approval, and sparingly. His moments of satisfaction revolved chiefly around how many horses were having brands changed and how well his men were presently doing in the business of dealing stolen horses. No matter how fast they moved stock, he never seemed satisfied.

Hays was scowling once again, as he and his men arrived with the new horses. His attitude should have been better. He had done well selling the stolen Montana horses to a Canadian ranch owner. All thirty of them in one place, for good money, no questions asked.

The taking of the replacements had been simple raids, with little trouble. The gang had stolen the horses from two operations just across the border. The only resistance had been from a boy who yelled for them to stop. Hays had shot the boy from his saddle.

Hays's anger grew as he approached the cabins. He didn't see his big gray mule grazing with the horse herd. That was his prize pack animal. He had intended to load up with supplies right away and begin another raid. What was keeping the four men he had sent to Fort Benton for supplies?

He dismounted and had one of his men take his horse for a rubdown. The outlaw leader was tall, with bony cheeks and deep-set, pale blue eyes. He wore a dark cotton shirt and a worn buckskin vest dotted with empty cartridge shells. For each man he had killed, he had saved the empty shell and had sewed it onto the vest.

Carson Hays rarely smiled. His humor usually came at the expense of another man's life. He had a slanted grin that emerged when he shot somebody. As he stood in front of the two cabins, he looked like he wanted to shoot somebody.

"You did real good, Carson," Lonnie said with a wide grin. "Good horses, and lots of them." His younger brother, Jeff, mimicked him with the same type of nervous smile.

Carson Hays ignored the warm welcome. "Where's the four men I sent to Fort Benton? They should have been back way before now."

Lonnie toyed with the buttons on his faded cotton shirt, intimidated by his older brother. He was a good three inches shorter than Carson and hated to look up into his brother's hard eyes.

"I was just about to send somebody to check on them," Lonnie finally said. "I don't know what's keeping them."

"I told them not to go whoring and gambling," Carson said strongly. "Damn them, anyway."

"I don't think they would do that," Jeff offered. "Not after you told them to come right back."

Jeff and Lonnie were about the same height, but Jeff was much slimmer. His clothes hung like bags on him. He glanced at Lonnie for support.

"Jeff's right," Lonnie said. "They wouldn't do that when you said to come right back."

"Then what's keeping them?" Carson impatiently demanded.

Jeff looked to his brother Lonnie, who could provide no more support, nor any satisfactory answer to Carson's question.

"*Well?*" Carson continued, his fists resting on his hips.

"Maybe they ran into trouble, Carson," Lonnie finally suggested. "That could have happened."

"Not if they stayed out of the saloons," Carson insisted. "By damn, if they didn't listen to what I told them—"

"They'll be back," Lonnie said. "Probably tonight."

"They've got until tonight to get back," Carson said. "If I have to go after them, they'll be damn sorry, all four of them."

"Come inside and have some beef and beans," Lonnie told his brother. "They'll be back."

Carson led the way into the main cabin and sat down to a rough board table. Lonnie took a big Dutch oven from the stove and ladled generous helpings into crystal plates for all three of them. They had stolen the crystal with some other items being freighted into Rocky Point the spring before, but Jeff had broken all of the glasses and all but four of the plates. He was no longer allowed to handle the dinnerware.

"We ain't got time to wait up for them fools," Carson said through a mouthful of food. "That Fourth of July gathering in Rocky Point is just two days away. Will Carlson will have his roan stallion there. I want that horse. I've always wanted that horse."

Lonnie looked at Jeff, who said nothing and looked back down at his plate. Will Carlson was a local rancher with some of the best horses in the badlands. Carson had long desired his best horse.

"Will Carlson's an edgy man," Lonnie pointed out, poking his fork through his food nervously. "He'll know for sure it was us who took him. It really ain't worth blowing this whole operation over one stupid horse."

"It ain't a stupid horse!" Carson yelled. "It's the best damned runner in this area."

Lonnie had been arguing with Carson for months about the idea of stealing Will Carlson's roan stallion. Smart thieves didn't steal from next door, no matter the quality. It was too dangerous. But no one argued with Carson and won.

"I want that horse," Carson insisted.

After the meal, Carson got up and went out to fume again in the twilight. He roamed around the cabins, looking up the trail for signs of incoming riders. He finally decided the four who had been sent to Fort Benton were quitting the gang. They would leave permanently, and he would send them off personally.

Later, in his bunk, Carson Hays continued to fret. He tossed and turned and finally got up and dressed in the moonlight. He walked out into the night to where the horses were grazing peacefully. The badlands were filled with eerie shadows as the moon overhead faded in and out of tattered clouds.

A lot of horses had come into the hideout while Hays was away and had been branded again for sale in Canada. Hays had connections both in Canada and in the Dakotas. The men he sold to would in turn move the horses to various military establishments, where horses were always in demand.

Hays's mind then turned to another train of thought that was always in the back of his mind. There was a woman who had deserted him, had run off and left him. Her note had said she would never see him again. Carson Hays had shot the note to bits. He kept the bullet-riddled pieces in a small wooden box that had been Lanna's, along with the wedding ring she had left behind.

Lanna was dark and lean and the prettiest thing he had ever seen in his life. She had been no more than a girl when he found her, eager to escape from a foster home in the Virginia City gold camps. She was wild and hearty and built for the trails. All she ever wanted, she had told him, was to be off by herself and away from the madness of crowds.

He thought again of how quickly she had taken to the

badlands. They were married within a month. Marriage was something he had never considered until Lanna. He had managed to convince her, at least for a time, that everyone but he and the men he chose needed to be robbed. He had taken her with him on many of his excursions into crime, although she had begged him to give it up. It was something he would never do.

Hays recalled their arguments. She threatened to leave him if he didn't give up thieving. He hadn't taken her seriously. Then the day came when he returned to the hideout with his brothers and a herd of stolen horses only to find Lanna gone.

She had shot one of the gang members who had tried to prevent her leaving. Her note said she would shoot anyone who tried to haul her back into the hideout.

Carson Hays vowed he would someday get Lanna back; either that or kill her. She would never belong to anyone else; she was his and his alone. He thought now that as long as he was going to have to go to Fort Benton, he would take the time to search some of the trails in that country for the one woman he would never allow to leave him.

He would find her, and he would bring her back. He would leave Lonnie in charge of stealing Will Carlson's roan stallion.

Hays turned from the grazing horses and stormed back to the main cabin, bursting through the door.

"Jeff!" he yelled, shaking his brother awake. "Jeff, go saddle that big bay for me. Get moving!"

Lonnie, awakened by the noise, sat up in his bunk. He listened to Carson tell him to roust four of the men from their bunks. "Tell them they're going to Fort Benton with me."

"Right now?"

Carson grabbed his brother by the hair and tilted his head up to look squarely into his tired eyes. "Yes, Lonnie, I said right now. You figure out how to get that roan stallion for me. I want to see that horse in the herd when I get back, understand?"

Carson Hays didn't wait for his brother to nod that he understood. He had already turned around and was out the door.

3

LASSITER RODE OUT of Fort Benton across a broad, grassy bench, leaving behind the wide flow of the Missouri to take a short cut. Soon he was in the heart of the badlands. To the south rose a small range of mountains called the Highwoods. A large, flat-topped butte stood out that was used as a landmark throughout the central part of Montana Territory.

The badlands were filled with pockets and swales where thieves and road agents could den up in wolfers' cabins and line shacks. Here a man made his own law and order. Lassiter guessed the Hays Gang knew every inch of this country.

The summer sun beat hot on the steep hills and coulees, the clay looking dark and smooth from a recent rain. The grass grew green in patches, wherever it could find a foothold. The clay mixed with the lighter grays of sagebrush and saltbush. In nearly every draw, Lassiter spooked herds of mule deer, their tawny hide blending with the rough country.

Late evening brought Lassiter to a good flow of water that he followed north, back toward the Missouri. At its bank, Lassiter spotted two men confronting an older man, who appeared to be tied to the railing of the ferry. The pair thrust a map in the old man's face. As Lassiter approached, the two stepped back casually, as if they had no reason to answer to anyone for what they were doing.

Lassiter observed the two men as he eased his stallion forward. One was blond-haired and cautious. He couldn't be a lot older than the outlaw Lassiter had encountered just out of Fort Benton. The other was middle-aged, with a face sunken on one side, as if his jaw had been badly broken and never healed properly. He had an itchy hand that hung near the butt of his revolver.

With a cool confidence, Lassiter reined in his stallion and ignored the two men. "You operate this ferry?" he asked the old man.

The old man, white-haired and frail in appearance, looked up at Lassiter as if he were crazy. He didn't even try to struggle against his bonds. How could he ignore the two men who were scowling at him? Lassiter just leaned across the saddle and smiled at him.

"If you do, I'd like to cross."

"You just ride on, mister," the broken-jawed one said. "We got business going on here."

"I've got business with him first," Lassiter informed him. "I need to cross the river."

The falling sun glistened off the river, painting one side of Lassiter's face in scarlet. The broken-jawed one studied Lassiter, then looked to the blond outlaw, as if he needed confirmation that he had support when the shooting started. But the blond was looking at Lassiter's twin Colts, and he began to get even more wary.

"Why don't we just come back later, Jed?" he suggested to the broken-jawed one. "We'll let this stranger cross. Then we'll visit old Charlie again."

The broken-jawed one grumbled and stuffed the map in a shirt pocket. The two of them then turned for their horses.

"Better watch them," the old man cautioned Lassiter. "They'll bushwhack you."

"No they won't," Lassiter said, getting down from his stallion. He yelled to them, "Untie this old man first."

The broken-jawed one turned to Lassiter, his face harder than ever.

"What did you say?"

"I said, untie him." Lassiter motioned toward the old man with his left thumb, allowing his right hand to hang near the butt of one Colt revolver. "I haven't got all day."

The broken-jawed outlaw looked to the blond, then the two of them started forward. Suddenly, the broken-jawed one reached for his gun, but Lassiter had a Colt cleared and fired into the man's chest twice before he even began to bring his pistol out of its holster. The blond outlaw's mouth dropped, and he began backing up with his hands in the air.

"I don't want no trouble, mister," he stammered. "It wasn't my idea to come here. It was his. Just let me go."

"Don't come back here ever again," Lassiter warned. "If you do, I'll know about it."

The blond outlaw hurried to his horse and was quickly lost in the late evening shadows of the trees along the river. Lassiter untied the old man before going over to see if the other outlaw was dead.

"Your neighbors aren't too friendly out here," Lassiter said casually, turning the outlaw's body over with his boot.

"That don't seem to matter none to you," the old man said, stretching his sore muscles. "You could handle just about anything, I'd have to say. Folks around here know me as Old Charlie. I'm much obliged to you, whoever you are."

"The name is Lassiter."

Charlie ambled over from the landing to where he kept a coffeepot on the coals near a fallen cottonwood log. He looked at Lassiter and pointed to the coffee before he sat down.

Lassiter accepted the offer and watched Charlie fill a tin cup for him. "Where am I?" Lassiter asked him.

Charlie pulled a corncob pipe from his pocket with a packet of tobacco. "You're at Clagett's Landing." He lit the pipe and pointed up from the river. "You know, there was once a pretty strong fort there, and there's still Sioux Injuns around here, but nothing seems to stop those damned horse thieves from doing just about anything they want."

"They were horse thieves?" Lassiter asked him. "You knew them?"

"They cross here off and on," Charlie replied, puffing on the pipe. "Never do pay the fee. But I ain't about to ask them for it."

"You ever heard of a man named Carson Hays?"

Charlie raised his eyebrows. "Carson Hays? He's the reason those two owlhoots had me tied to the ferry's rail. They're after a woman who used to be his wife."

"Then you know him?"

"Not any more than I care to know. But like I said, in these parts there ain't much but their kind around."

Lassiter went over to the dead outlaw and took the map from his body. It was a crude, hand-drawn outline of the river and the badlands around it for some distance. Near the middle of the map was Clagett's Landing, with a series of small x's in heavy pencil along a drainage called Arrow Creek.

Lassiter returned to the log and handed the map to Charlie.

"What did they want from you?" Lassiter asked him.

"I know these parts pretty well," Charlie said, studying the map and sucking hard on his pipe. "Them two brought this map to me and wanted me to show them where I thought Carson Hays's woman was hiding out. Those little x's are cabins up and down Arrow Creek. Carson and his gang think I know which one of those cabins his woman is hiding out in."

"And I suppose you do," Lassiter suggested.

Charlie smiled through a cloud of pipe smoke. "Damned tootin' I do. But I ain't about to let them know."

Lassiter reached into his pocket and pulled out the picture of Lorna Jackson and her husband. "You know her?" he said, pointing to the woman.

'Why, that's Lanna Hays!" Charlie blurted. "She's all dressed up. But that ain't Carson Hays there with her."

"I'll tell you something," Lassiter said to Charlie. "That woman in the picture isn't Lanna Hays. It's her twin sister, Lorna."

"What?"

"Yes, identical twins. I came out here looking for Lorna Jackson, the woman in the picture. She came out here in the first place to find her twin sister, Lanna. But I've got to find Lorna before we can both go look for Lanna."

Charlie scratched his head. "I'll be a gut-shot buffalo," he said, laughing. "If that doesn't beat all."

"Lorna Jackson, the woman I want to find, came this way with a mule skinner. She's headed for Rocky Point."

"That's smack-dab in the middle of Hays country," Charlie said, pouring himself and Lassiter more coffee.

"The Hays boys got a hideout just north of there, in the badlands where nobody wants to go."

"Well, I guess I'm going to have to go there," Lassiter said.

"How in hell's name did you get mixed up in all this?" Charlie wanted to know.

"I've got a friend laid up in Fort Benton who got shot up by some of the Hays gang," Lassiter said. "You might say I'm looking for this woman as a favor to him."

The old man chuckled. "What a man won't do for a friend. A woman or a friend."

Lassiter studied the map. "I came across that creek a ways back," Lassiter told Charlie. "That's rough country."

"You could hide almost anything you wanted to in there," Charlie said. He looked at the map with Lassiter and pointed a finger. "If I was to guess, I'd say she's back up here, where she can see the country in all directions."

"You know that area pretty well, don't you?" Lassiter said.

"I ought to," Charlie said, puffing. "I hunted wolves in there for three years."

"Sounds to me like this country is filling up with a different kind of wolf now," Lassiter said, folding the map.

"That's for sure," Charlie said with a nod. "If you go looking for Lanna Hays, you'd better watch yourself. Folks say there's not many who can stand up to her, no more than the man she married."

"Is she stealing livestock on her own?" Lassiter wondered.

"I couldn't say." Charlie was stoking his pipe with a grass stem. "I don't know what she's doing. All I know is she was married to Carson Hays and used to ride with him and his brothers. She learned a lot from them. I hope you don't have to shoot her, too."

"I've never shot a woman before," Lassiter told him. "I won't start now."

Charlie squinted. "There's always a first time."

"If she's that bad," Lassiter asked him, "why didn't you want to tell those two who tied you up where you thought she was hiding?"

Charlie looked at Lassiter and puffed on his pipe. "It's the principle of the thing, you see. Now, if they would have asked me in a nice way—"

Lassiter smiled. "You're one for manners. I can see that."

"I don't care how bad she is," Charlie continued. "She don't bother me a'tall. But them Hays boys and their bunch are more than I can stand. So they can take their own chances with her."

"If she's hiding out, she must want to quit the bunch, don't you think?"

"That's most likely," Charlie acknowledged. "But you can't be too sure about her."

"You paint her to be worse than any of the Hays Gang," Lassiter said.

Charlie nodded. "All except one. Carson Hays is s'posed to be a fast man with a gun. Some say he's likely to never be beat." He looked at Lassiter and winked. "But I don't put much faith in the word *never*."

Lassiter got up from the cottonwood log and thanked Charlie for the coffee.

"You'd just as well stay here the night," Charlie offered. "You can't see much in these badlands after dark."

"Thanks just the same," Lassiter said, "but I'm going to ride on."

"You ain't heard all my stories yet," Charlie protested. "I got lots of them. We could swap some."

"Some other time," Lassiter said, putting the map in

his saddlebag. "I would, but I've got to get to Rocky Point as fast as I can. I thank you for the information."

"I'm more obliged to you than you are to me," the old man said. He stood up and relit his pipe. "I've never been around Carson Hays, but I can say that I've never seen a man shoot like you before." He pointed to the dead outlaw.

"You want me to help bury him?" Lassiter asked. "I should have asked before."

Charlie laughed. "Bury him? Hell, I plan to use him for catfish bait."

Lassiter nodded. "Suit yourself."

"You want his gun and horse?" Charlie asked.

"Keep them. In my opinion, you earned them. Is there an easy trail through these badlands to Rocky Point?"

Charlie looked again through twilight at Lassiter's two big Colts. "There's no easy trail anywhere through these badlands. Rocky Point's on the north bank, but it don't matter which side you ride on. You can cross over to Rocky Point easy, once you get there. The only deep water is where the steamboats pull in."

"Anything else I should know?" Lassiter asked him.

"Don't get too far off the main freight road or you'll miss Rocky Point and end up at Carroll," Charlie advised.

Lassiter tipped his hat. "I hope someone comes along soon to listen to your stories."

Charlie laughed. "I hope you find that woman who looks like Lanna Hays, and then Lanna Hays herself," he said before Lassiter left. "When the Hays Gang comes back here to talk to me again, I'd like to be able to say there's no reason for them to look for nobody. I'd like to be able to tell them to go to hell, 'cause that's where they'll be headed if they run across a stranger dressed in black."

4

LONNIE HAYS WATCHED the sun rise with his younger brother, Jeff, from the entrance to the main cabin. Both men were tired, but the cool breeze that came down the canyon refreshed them. They watched the men saddling horses while the early light chased the shadows out of the deep pockets and swales around the hideout. It was going to be a very busy day.

After Carson had left for Fort Benton, one of the men on lookout had reported seeing three riders who had looked down on the hideout and then rode away. Everyone knew it was only a matter of time until their lair was discovered, but the timing couldn't be worse. Carson was gone and the Fourth of July celebration in Rocky Point would soon be under way. Now three men knew the bandits' location, and they would likely tell others.

Because of this, Lonnie felt he couldn't afford to leave the hideout to go into Rocky Point for the Fourth of July cele-bration. It was hard to say when the men would return, or even if they would. But Lonnie thought they would be back.

He certainly didn't want to leave all the horses unguarded. Jeff and two men were scheduled to go and covertly maneuver Will Carlson's roan stallion out of town, along with any other horses that were easy prey.

"Just take the roan if that's the only horse you can get easily," Lonnie emphasized. "Carson wants that horse for certain. We've got to make him happy."

"He always wanted something that was real hard to come by," Jeff said disgustedly. "Just like that woman he married. He lost her, but he still won't let well enough alone with her."

"That's none of our concern," Lonnie told his brother.

"It is so," Jeff argued. "He'll be off chasing around looking for her while he's over at Fort Benton. You know that as well as me."

"It still don't concern us," Lonnie said again.

Jeff wouldn't let it go. He kicked his boot through the loose dirt beside the cabin. "I wished he'd just forget about her and find some other woman, if that's what he wants. She's holed up somewhere and can't be found."

"She's been found," Lonnie said in disagreement. "Remember when Price and Les and Jack went to look for her?"

"They never came back."

"That's what I mean," Lonnie said with a nod. "She's been found, but she likely shot them, all three. She said she'd do it in her note."

"How'd they know where she was?"

"We'll never know."

"I know I ain't never going to find a woman like that for myself," Jeff said, watching the sun clear a giant bald knob of gumbo clay across the canyon. "But you know, I kind of think she took a shine to me."

"What are you talking about?"

Jeff smiled sheepishly. "She used to talk nice to me all the time," he replied. "She used to ask me why I didn't think of changing my life. I think she kind of liked me."

"Don't ever tell Carson that. He'll kill you."

"I ain't about to tell Carson nothing about that. I just wished I'd met her first."

"Carson would have taken her away from you," Lonnie pointed out. "She's Carson's woman."

"Maybe so," Jeff said, "but I still think she likes me. And if I was to ever see her again, I'd like to find out for sure. Maybe she'd go off with me somewhere."

"That's crazy talk. Carson would find you and tear you into little bitty pieces."

"I suppose you're right," Jeff said. "But I do like to think about her, anyway."

"That ain't right," Lonnie said. "You'd ought to take Smiley and Gruber and get going."

"What about those three that Gruber saw looking down here?" Jeff asked.

"I've got enough men staying back here with me to handle that," Lonnie said. "I wish them same three would come back. We could take care of them and not have to worry anymore."

Jeff kicked in the dirt again. "I don't like it, Lonnie. Maybe we'd ought to think about moving our hideout."

"We'll talk it over with Carson when he gets back," Lonnie said. "We'll make it so he thinks it was his idea. Now, get going for Rocky Point. Be careful, but make sure you get that horse."

Rocky Point was a small cluster of log buildings bunched together on the north banks of the Missouri. Lassiter reached the town near midday, after finding a place in the badlands to camp and catch up on his sleep. He knew he was going to need all the energy he could muster before everything was all over.

The town was celebrating. People jammed the dusty street, spilling drinks at their feet while they laughed and danced to the music of two fiddlers. Since leaving Fort Benton, Lassiter hadn't been keeping track of the days. The merriment told him it was the Fourth of July.

He hadn't expected to have to comb through this kind of crowd to find Lorna Jackson. Though normally there were very few women this far out from established schools and churches, a good number had just gotten off a steamboat headed for Fort Benton. They lined the street with their husbands waiting for an upcoming horse race.

Lassiter was most interested in locating the freighters that had come into Rocky Point. He counted three outfits on the edge of town, their goods already unloaded. The bullwhackers and mule skinners were no doubt celebrating in the streets with the others.

Lassiter worked his way through the crowd and the two log saloons, looking for the drivers. He found two of them and showed them Lorna Jackson's picture. They both told him the same thing: no woman had ridden out with them from Fort Benton.

The third driver was helping a man shoe a sleek roan stallion he was entering in the horse race. The driver was short and stocky, with sky blue suspenders holding up worn pants. Over his thick graying hair he wore a faded green derby with a crow's feather on the left side. He pulled on his suspenders and spit out a stream of tobacco juice as he addressed Lassiter.

"Jake Broden is my name," he said by way of introduction. "This here is Will Carlson. He's about to win the race on this roan of his."

Carlson turned and shook hands with Lassiter. He was a

small, middle-aged man with quick motions, who studied Lassiter with equally quick glances.

"Glad to meet you. What are you, a gunfighter?"

"I wear them in case I need them."

"I'll bet."

"I'd say you have a better than even chance on a horse like that," Lassiter told Carlson.

"You intend to race?" Carlson asked Lassiter. "I saw you ride in on a fine stallion of your own."

"Not today," Lassiter said. "I'm looking for a woman who came into town with a freight driver." He showed the two men the picture of Lorna Jackson.

"She come out here with me all right," Jake acknowledged, spitting more tobacco juice. "Said she was to meet her sister here. Never did say her name, though. Oddest woman I ever did see. Mannerly, but odd."

"She has amnesia," Lassiter explained.

"Am—what?"

"Amnesia, an affliction. She has trouble remembering who she is at times. She's lost."

Jake nodded. "I didn't do anything but call her ma'am. I ain't one to harm women. She was nice and asked for a ride, so I gave her one. First time that ever happened. A right nice gal."

"Do you know where she is now?" Lassiter asked.

"She told me her sister was coming to town, and she had to get a room at the hotel. That was the last I talked to her." Then the mule skinner pointed into the crowd. "I saw that older woman, the one with the blue and pink bonnet, talking with her yesterday after she left me. She might be able to help."

"Thanks, Jake," Lassiter said quickly. He extended his best wishes in the horse race to Will Carlson and strolled toward an older woman standing with two younger ladies.

Lassiter approached them and removed his hat. "Please excuse me," he began, "but maybe you ladies could be of some help to me."

"I'm not sure how," the older woman said.

Lassiter showed her the picture. "I'm trying to locate that woman, and I understand she might have spoken with you yesterday."

The two younger women covered their mouths with their hands and began giggling. The older woman frowned at them, and they immediately brought themselves under control.

"Yes, we've seen that woman, and I talked with her briefly," she told Lassiter. "She seems a nice sort, and dresses well. But the way she travels— She came into town on a freight wagon. My word." The two younger women began giggling again.

"She probably doesn't even know where she is," Lassiter told them. "She has amnesia and is lost up here." Lassiter tapped his temple.

The older woman covered her mouth. "Oh, my goodness. I'm so sorry."

"Did she tell you anything about where she was going?" Lassiter asked.

"I didn't ask her anything that was none of my business," the woman made clear. "I just asked her if I could be of help in any way, and she said she was looking for her sister. I didn't know the name, so I couldn't tell her anything that would help her."

"You wouldn't have any idea where she might be now?" Lassiter asked.

"None whatsoever. But I did overhear some of the other ladies talking about a strange woman wandering around down by the steamboat."

"How long ago was that?" Lassiter asked.

"Couldn't have been more than an hour ago or so," the woman answered.

Lassiter tipped his hat and hurried off the main street, down to where the steamboat was docked. There were a few people milling about on the deck and a few on shore. Near a crude loading dock were parked three wagons in single file. Hitched to the front wagon was a team of a dozen mules, Jake Broden's outfit.

A dark-haired woman with her hair loose, wearing a light blue cotton dress trimmed with lace, sat on the tailgate of the last wagon, swinging her legs and looking out across the river. A blue bonnet lay next to her, and a small leather satchel rested in the wagon behind her.

Lassiter removed his hat and approached the woman slowly.

"Mrs. Jackson? Mrs. Lorna Jackson?"

The woman turned with a blank expression in her brown eyes. She was even prettier than her image in the picture. Lassiter could see she had no idea whose name he had just called her by.

"I guess I didn't hear you," the woman said. "Were you looking for somebody?"

Lassiter pulled out the picture. He showed it to the woman. "Do you recognize that man, Darren Jackson, your husband?" he asked. "And yourself, standing beside him?"

Lorna Jackson grew startled and looked up at Lassiter. "How did you get that picture?" she asked.

"No need to worry," Lassiter told her. "My name is Lassiter, and I've come on behalf of your husband and a friend of mine to take you home. Kansas City is a long way from here."

"Oh, my goodness," she said. "I can't go back. Not yet. Not until I find my twin sister."

"It's not going to be easy to find her, you realize."

Lorna then became stern, and her face hardened. "I really don't know you, Mr. Lassiter, but I want you to understand that I'm going to stay as long as it takes to find Lanna. She should be down in Kansas City living with me."

"What if she doesn't want to go down to Kansas City with you?"

"That won't be a problem, Mr. Lassiter," Lorna said. "I know she has been wondering about me for many years. Do you understand, Mr. Lassiter?"

Lassiter nodded. "I suggest we should get started. I have an idea where she might be. I got some information and a map from an old ferry operator back along the river."

"You know where she is?" Lorna asked, her hopes rising.

"Just an idea of where she is." He produced the map and told her about the incident at Clagett's Landing, noting that she took the story in with great interest, including the part about his having had to shoot one of the outlaws.

"You appear to be a man who knows how to use a gun," Lorna told him. "I could see that right away. I'd rather be fighting with you than against you."

"Have you ever had to fight before?" Lassiter asked her.

"I've never killed anyone, if that's what you mean," she answered. "But, yes, I have shot a man before."

Lassiter didn't ask her the circumstances. "Do you realize your sister used to be married to an outlaw?" Lassiter asked her. "She used to ride with a bunch called the Hays Gang."

Lorna didn't look at him, but stared out across the Missouri instead. "I don't know what her troubles are," she said blankly. "But I can feel she isn't doing well."

34

"I told you, I learned she is an outlaw," Lassiter pressed. "She could be dangerous."

"Nonsense, Mr. Lassiter," Lorna said, turning back quickly. "She's no more dangerous than I am. You can be certain of that."

"No more dangerous than you?"

"No more dangerous than me," Lorna said with a nod.

"How dangerous is that?" Lassiter asked.

"I don't start problems, and I'm not fond of trouble," she answered, "but rest assured that if someone wills me harm, they had better look out."

5

THE DAY WAS GETTING WARMER, and the sounds of the celebration grew louder. Lassiter studied Lorna as she once again stared out across the river. It seemed all too obvious that she would resist any attempt to get her to go back without her sister, no matter the danger.

"We should get started looking for your sister," Lassiter finally said. "The sooner we locate her, the sooner you both can get back home."

"I am home. I know I'm home. Aren't I?"

"You live in Kansas City, Mrs. Jackson. You've got to go back down there."

"Why would I ride down there?" Lorna asked. "Lanna is here, isn't she? I thought she was here, in Rocky Point."

"What made you think she would be here?" Lassiter asked her. He was wondering if she had seen this country as a child.

"I don't know," Lorna replied. "It just feels like we've been here before, Lanna and I."

"Maybe you came through here in a wagon as a little girl," Lassiter suggested.

"I don't know," Lorna said, "I don't remember. That was so long ago."

Lassiter knew these badlands were a long ways north of the Oregon Trail, but Ben Morris hadn't made it clear where the people she grew up with had settled. Then Lassiter began to understand that, as identical twins, it was possible that Lorna was feeling what Lanna felt about this country, since Lanna had no doubt lived here for some time.

Though he was no doctor, and even doctors couldn't answer every question, Lassiter knew that identical twins sometimes acted and thought very much the same. In this case, Lorna and her sister, Lanna, had been separated for so long that they couldn't be living in the same way. But there was certainly the possibility of their feeling like each other.

To Lassiter, it didn't really matter what had happened in Lorna's head to steer her way up here; it was important to get her out of the area right away and on the way back to Fort Benton. From there, her husband could be notified, and Ben Morris could get her back down to Kansas City.

"How will we travel?" Lorna asked.

"What I was going to suggest," Lassiter replied, "was that we see if we can find a horse for you. We should be able to do that. Then we can get started for this creek west of here, where your sister is supposed to be hiding out." He showed her the map.

"Let me see," Lorna said, and looked to where Lassiter pointed among the markings along Arrow Creek. "You think she's there somewhere?"

"That's the most likely place so far."

"But I thought I would surely find her here," Lorna said sadly. "I wish she was here."

"Not likely," Lassiter said. "She's hiding out from her husband, is what I've learned. She wouldn't want to be close to his hideout."

Lorna looked out across the river once again and brushed away a tear. "Sometimes I get so confused. I don't know who I am or where I'm supposed to be."

"Once we find your sister, we have to go back to Fort Benton and wire your husband," Lassiter told her. "I want to check in on my friend while I'm there. He was shot by members of the Hays Gang just a few days back."

"I didn't mean to be so much trouble," Lorna said. "But my husband thinks my fall is what's causing all this. Did you hear about my fall?"

"I heard," Lassiter told her.

"I was riding my horse, and she jumped a lilac hedge and stumbled. I fell and hit my head, and two weeks later I awakened and tried to run out of the room. Friends later told me I didn't know anybody, including myself. Despite that, I always know that I have to find Lanna."

Lassiter nodded in understanding. "It must have been a hard time for you, and everyone around you."

"It still is a hard time," she said. "I hope you will understand that in helping me find Lanna—that is, if you still intend to help me—"

"I intend to help," Lassiter said with a nod, folding the map. "I intend to help you find her just as quickly as we can."

Lassiter carried Lorna's satchel, and the two of them rejoined the crowd up at Rocky Point. Lassiter had hoped to get to talk to Jake Broden about buying a horse from someone and then getting some supplies, but the horse race was just getting under way, and the people were shouting and betting as they took positions to watch along the road at the edge of town.

"Let's stay and watch the race first," Lorna begged. "Then we can leave."

"I don't see why not," Lassiter said.

Lassiter drew a number of stares, as he always did, as he got into position with Lorna to watch. The race got under way, the course a long circle of nearly a mile that wound along the bluffs above the river. People pointed and clapped and cheered as the riders maneuvered their horses along the hills through clouds of dust.

As Lassiter looked around the crowd, he noticed three men off by themselves looking hard at him and Lorna.

"Have you seen those men before, Lorna?" Lassiter asked her.

"I don't know anyone here, Mr. Lassiter," Lorna said, keeping her eyes on the race. "I don't have any idea who they are."

The way the men were acting, Lassiter was almost certain they knew Lorna, or thought they did. Finally, when Lassiter returned their stares, they moved off into the crowd.

The finish was at the end of the short main street. Lorna stayed close to Lassiter as the horses thundered past them in a cloud of dust. She clapped and shouted with the others.

Will Carlson rode his roan stallion hard. In a tight finish, Carlson's roan edged past a big bay ridden by an older man, while the spectators clapped and jumped up and down.

"That was a good race," Lorna commented. "It makes

me remember my younger days. I hope we can find Lanna. I want to show her my horses.''

"I understand you can ride pretty well," Lassiter told Lorna.

"I can ride very well, thank you," Lorna said. "I was riding a horse most of the way up here, but somehow lost him near Fort Benton. That's why I rode on in the wagon."

"I see," Lassiter said. "You don't know how you lost your horse?"

"I can't remember," Lorna said. "Really, I can't remember."

"Why don't we look for Jake Broden now? Hopefully, he'll know someone we can get a horse from for you," Lassiter suggested.

"That is a good idea," Lorna said. "But I must confess, I have very little money left. If you will find a suitable horse and make a deal for me, I will certainly have my husband repay you when we find Lanna and get back down to Kansas City."

Lassiter nodded. He wasn't worried so much about the money; he knew he would be reimbursed. He just hoped Lorna would remember what she was saying about wanting to get back to Kansas City. Just moments ago, it seemed as if her mind had been back in her childhood. Now she was thinking as she normally would if she were with her husband in Kansas City. He hoped it would stay that way.

Jake Broden was congratulating Will Carlson when Lassiter and Lorna approached him about looking for a horse. Jake smiled when he saw Lorna.

"I liked your company, ma'am," he told her. "You made the trip out here a lot more interesting." He pulled on his suspenders and nodded.

Lorna had a puzzled look on her face. "Who are you?" she asked.

Jake blinked. "You rode all the way out here with me, don't you remember?"

"We haven't met before," Lorna said. "I don't know you."

"You rode on my wagon," Jake said again.

Lorna looked at Jake and blinked. "Oh my, yes, I do remember now. Please forgive me."

Jake looked at Lassiter and back to Lorna. "Think nothing of it, ma'am."

"I have to thank you for your kindness in allowing the lady to travel with you," Lassiter told him. "I was hoping to ask you for one more favor."

"I'll do my best," Jake said with a nod.

"We need a good, strong saddle horse," Lassiter explained. "You know a lot of the people around here. Do you suppose any of them would want to sell us a horse?"

"I could look into it," Jake promised. "Give me a little time, and I'll see what I can do."

Will Carlson then spoke up. "I think I could sell you one of my horses at a pretty good price," he said to Lorna. "If you and Mr. Lassiter would like to come out to my ranch with me when the festivities are over, you could look my horses over and decide for yourself."

"That would be very nice, thank you," Lorna said.

Lassiter realized they likely wouldn't be able to get a horse from anybody until the celebrating was over anyway, and Will Carlson had offered. It would be best to just enjoy the day and get going after the festivities.

"I'll look you up when I get ready to go back," Carlson said. "Right now, I've got some money to collect."

"Thank you very much," Lorna said with a smile.

Carlson left, his small, thin frame stretched upward in pride. Lassiter couldn't help wondering how his own stallion would have fared in the race.

"You should have entered that stallion of yours," Jake said. "Who knows, Carlson might not be so cocky right now."

"My horse went through some rough country getting here," Lassiter said. "I don't think a race like that would have been too good."

Jake smiled. "Who you trying to kid? That horse is fitter than any of them that was in the race, including Carlson's roan."

Lassiter smiled. "Well, let's just say I wasn't in a racing mood today."

"That's good enough for me," Jake said, adjusting his green derby. "How about if I treat you both to a plate of that fried chicken over yonder?" He pointed to a line of tables where people were taking seats to be served. "I'm plumb starved."

Lorna and Lassiter agreed they could use a good meal. They walked with Jake over to where the crowd was congregating, found seats, and were soon served plates stacked high with chicken. The fiddlers started in again and dancers crowded the area just beyond the tables.

Partway through the meal, Lorna was asked to dance. The man asking was young and rowdy-looking, and Lassiter immediately recognized him as one of the men who had been staring at them during the horse race.

"I guess just one wouldn't hurt," Lorna said.

"She hasn't finished her meal yet," Lassiter told the young ruffian.

"I didn't ask you, mister," he growled at Lassiter. "Butt out."

Lassiter rose to his feet and Lorna stepped between

them. "I'll dance one, quick dance with him," she said. "There's no harm in that."

"You don't have to, Lorna," Lassiter told her. "Why would you even want to?"

Lorna looked at Lassiter and her expression turned glassy. "I like to dance," she finally said.

"Not today," Lassiter told her.

"What did I tell you about butting in?" the young rowdy said.

"How would you like to be taken down to size?" Lassiter asked him.

"You're going to do it?" he asked Lassiter.

"It would be a pleasure."

"No, don't," Lorna begged Lassiter. "I'll dance a quick dance with him. Just one. I'll be right back."

Lassiter shook his head. "It's not a good idea, Lorna," he tried again.

"I'll be right back," she insisted.

The young rowdy gloated as he left the table with Lorna in hand and moved toward the crowd of dancers. Lassiter noticed the two other men who had been staring at them earlier watching him from a distance. He turned toward them, and they angled off into the crowd.

Jake was watching it all with a look of concern. "You'd best go get her if she don't come back real quick," he warned Lassiter. "She's in bad company, *real* bad company."

"Who is that?" Lassiter asked.

"Jeff Hays. He's one of a gang of brothers who hang out around here."

"One of Carson Hays's gang?" Lassiter asked.

"The same bunch," Jake said with a nod. "He's the youngest brother. How'd you know about them?"

43

"I believe I met some of them the first day I got to Fort Benton," Lassiter told him. "And I've been meeting more of them almost every day since I started out into this country. I'd better get her away from him before it's too late."

6

"I FIGURED you'd dance with me," Jeff Hays told Lorna as he reeled her around among the other dancers. "You've always been partial to me, huh?"

Lorna stared at him, trying to understand why he was talking to her that way.

"You act like you don't even know me," the young outlaw finally told Lorna. His eyes held a wild look, and his grin showed dark, uneven teeth. "This is the first time I ever seen you dressed up like you are. *Ain't* you something?"

"What are you talking about?" Lorna asked. "I don't know you."

Jeff Hays laughed. "You trying to play some kind of trick? I can't figure why you came down to Rocky Point. You should have known Carson or one of us would find you here. But I'm glad you did."

Lorna's eyes widened as she finally understood what the outlaw was saying. He had mistaken her for Lanna, her twin sister. It was no wonder he thought it strange that she would be out in the open celebrating the Fourth of July when she was on the run from his older brother.

"I guess you figure on going back with me to see Carson, then?" Jeff said to her.

Lorna realized she should have listened to Lassiter's advice. She'd have to act immediately if she was going to get out of this strange, serious situation.

"We'd better be getting back to Mr. Lassiter," she said. "He and I have to be leaving soon."

"Who is he, anyway?" Jeff held her tighter, forcing her to continue dancing.

"He's a friend," Lorna told him.

"How *good* a friend?"

Lorna tried to work herself loose. "I want to go back now. Thank you for the dance."

"You ain't going back to him, you ought to know that," Jeff said, clutching her harder. "I found you, and I'm taking you back to Carson. Right now!"

Jeff dragged Lorna from the group of dancers, in the opposite direction from Lassiter. She swung her head around and saw him scanning the crowd for her. But she couldn't get his attention as Jeff Hays pulled her from the gathering of people and off toward the trees.

"Where do you think you're taking me?" Lorna demanded, pulling back against him.

"I told you, you're going back to Carson," Jeff answered. "What do you think, I'm going to just let you go back to that stranger in black?"

Lorna began to struggle harder. She tried to yell, but Hays closed a hand over her mouth and continued to drag her. He pulled her further into the woods along the river. The other two men were waiting for them on horseback, eager to get going. With them were five horses they had stolen, among them Will Carson's roan stallion.

"I got her," Jeff told the two, as he struggled with Lorna. "I told you I would."

"We've got to get going with these horses," said Smiley, an older outlaw with wire-thin lips. "Dance or no dance, Will Carlson is bound to miss his horse soon."

"Do you think I should have left her?" Jeff Hays asked.

"You should have let Carson come get her," Smiley said.

"Carson ain't here," Jeff Hays snapped. "What kind of thing is that to say? Now, get off your horse and help me here."

Smiley reluctantly climbed down from his horse. He was frowning and looking back past Jeff Hays, back through the trees.

"What's the matter with you?" Hays asked him. "Hurry up!"

"Someone's bound to come," Smiley said. "We ain't got a chance if a bunch of them show up."

"I can hardly believe Lanna would be dressed like that," Gruber, the other outlaw, commented, shaking his head in disbelief. "Who would have known? But there she is, plain as day."

"She acted like she didn't even know who I was," Jeff said, trying to get Lorna close to his horse.

Lorna began to struggle furiously, angering Jeff Hays all the more. He took his hand from her mouth to strike her and she began to yell. He covered her mouth once again and swore into her ear.

Smiley stepped nervously as he held Jeff's horse. He turned to Gruber. "Start them horses out of here," he ordered. "We'll catch up."

"You ain't giving no orders here!" Jeff yelled. "We'll all go together. What if he runs into somebody?"

"Jeff, they'll be coming any time," Smiley pleaded.

Jeff Hays had Lorna near his horse. "Get that rope from my saddle, and I'll tie her up good," Jeff told Smiley. "Carson will be happy with me."

Lorna struggled ever stronger, kicking Hays repeatedly along the lower legs and foot area. It did little good, as he wore thick boots. He just laughed.

"You sure don't want to go back, do you?" he said. "You shouldn't have come to Rocky Point."

Smiley had just gotten the rope loose when Lorna got a free hand on Jeff Hays's pistol. She pulled it from its holster and cocked it. Jeff Hays tried to pin her arm, but she pulled the trigger, and the bullet shattered his knee.

Jeff released Lorna and slumped to the ground, yelling and holding his wounded leg. Lorna backed away and cocked the pistol once again. Filled with pain and rage, Jeff struggled to rise. Lorna fired once again. The bullet narrowly missed the left side of his head. He ducked back and held his hands up.

Smiley dropped the rope and climbed onto his horse. He and Gruber then kicked their horses into a run, leaving Jeff and the five prize horses they had stolen.

"Come back here!" he yelled after them.

Lorna pulled the hammer back once again. She edged closer and closer to Hays, holding the pistol out in front, aimed at his head.

"Did you think you were going to kidnap me?" she asked Jeff. "Well, did you?"

"Don't shoot," he pleaded. He was fighting his fear and the pain that coursed through his entire left leg. "Just don't shoot."

Lorna stopped and lowered the gun just a fraction, deciding whether or not to use it. Hays put his hands on his bloody knee and began moaning. He looked up at her, and Lorna raised the pistol once more.

"I've decided I'll shoot you after all," Lorna told him.

Smiley Waller and Gruber rode as fast as they could away from Rocky Point. Waller was less worried about getting away from any angry townspeople than about what Lonnie Hays was going to say when he heard the news about his brother Jeff. And then what Carson Hays would say.

Waller was liked and respected among the gang members. He had gotten his nickname, Smiley, because of his thin, wide lips. He had gotten used to it, as he had gotten used to the Hays Gang and their ways. Five years with the gang had taught Waller that if anything went wrong, everyone but the Hays boys was to blame.

Waller had ridden with the gang at its formation. A failure in the gold fields, he had taken to the life of a road agent near Virginia City and Bannock. He had outlasted a few groups of vigilantes—they were referred to as stranglers in the badlands—before deciding to move on. He had become too easily recognized in the gold fields to have lasted much longer.

When he met the Hays boys, they had set up operations in the Dakotas. Later, just a year ago, they had moved into the Missouri badlands. He had put up with the Hays boys and their ways because he was fed right and didn't have to do a lot to keep them happy. Mainly, his job was to watch the horses around the hideout. After today, he didn't know what was going to happen.

Waller knew what had happened to Jeff Hays was going to change the gang forever. None of the three brothers had ever faced real trouble before, and essentially the badlands had been theirs. Other members of the gang had quit or, on occasion, had been killed during a raid. Two had been hanged the summer before by angry ranchers. But nothing had ever happened to the Hays boys themselves.

Waller knew what had just happened would have many repercussions. Jeff was likely dead or soon would be. The woman was back in their lives. The roan stallion was lost. Waller knew Carson Hays would be angriest about the woman and the horse.

He knew from experience that Carson Hays could pull a gun on a man and shoot him in the blink of an eye. Carson Hays had nearly killed him the day they met. Waller had picked up Carson's personal whiskey bottle. Intervention by Lonnie Hays had saved his life.

Lonnie was going to be livid now. He had been instructed by Carson to have that roan for him when he got back from Fort Benton. Waller knew Lonnie would blame him for everything, for not looking after his younger brother better and for losing the horse and Lanna. Waller wished now he had insisted on having Lonnie along and had left Jeff behind to watch the hideout with the others.

Waller and Gruber stopped their winded horses at the mouth of a deep draw to allow them to rest. Gruber found himself as worried as Waller, though he was far more valuable to their operations. Gruber was an expert at changing brands. He had worked for numerous gangs in the New Mexico and Colorado areas, until the gangs had been broken up—at least for a time—by angry stockgrowers who had organized into vigilante groups.

Gruber had barely escaped the wrath of ten angry ranchers. Only a quirk of fate had saved him from hanging with four others on a brisk autumn day in the mountains of northern New Mexico. The limb he had been dangling from had snapped at the same time the rest of the gang showed up to shoot it out with the ranchers. The gang had prevailed and Gruber still had the scars on his neck.

In New Mexico, Gruber had been blamed by the gang leader for the circumstances that led to their being caught by the stranglers. Though Gruber argued that he was not to blame, the leader wouldn't listen. Gruber had to flee that night in fear of his life.

As far as Gruber could see now, this situation was even graver. During his worst nightmare, the leader of the New Mexico gang could never have envisioned Carson Hays. As far as the Hays Gang was concerned, it didn't matter how good Gruber was at changing brands, he was expendable.

Waller and Gruber sat their exhausted horses and looked back toward Rocky Point. They watched for the dust of pursuers and finally decided no one had come after them.

"You suppose we'd ought to go back and try to get Jeff?" Gruber suggested.

"We'd get shot up," Waller replied. "Jeff's likely dead by now, anyhow."

"What if he ain't? We should at least try."

"It's too late. If we were going to get him out of there, we should have shot the woman. But you know how that would have set with Carson."

Both men knew they were in a no-win situation. They couldn't have brought Jeff Hays back with them without shooting the woman. They couldn't have remained without putting their own lives on the line. The only thing they could have done was ride out, and now they were going to have to pay for that as well.

"What will Lonnie say, us showing up without Jeff or the horses?" Gruber asked.

"It was Jeff's fault, that's plain," Waller emphasized. "There wasn't a thing we could do. I tried to help him, but she was too much for him. You saw it, didn't you?"

"Yeah, I saw it," Gruber acknowledged. "That don't mean Lonnie won't be plumb owly. And what will Carson say when he gets back?"

"Carson should have been in on this one," Waller said. "Did you see that man dressed in black, with the twin Colts? He's one to be reckoned with, I'd say."

"He couldn't stand up to Carson," Gruber said.

"Maybe not," Waller said with a shrug, "but something about him made me real wary. I don't know where he came from, but he was with Lanna. That means he could be real dangerous with a gun."

"That don't mean nothing," Gruber said, trying to make himself believe the leader of the gang he belonged to was untouchable. "Just because he took a shine to Lanna don't mean he can stand up to Carson."

"You think about it," Waller said. "He picks up with Lanna, and she tells him who Carson Hays is, and he stays with her anyway. Don't that tell you something?"

"Only that he's a fool."

"Or that he's good with a gun, or thinks he is. Either way it means big trouble."

"Carson'll take care of him," Gruber said again.

Waller looked at Gruber. "You and I had better hope Carson can take care of him. That stranger saw us with Jeff. He won't forget us, I'll wager you that. Carson had better oil his guns. Let's get going."

7

"DON'T SHOOT HIM, LORNA," Lassiter said. "Don't do it."

Lorna was glaring at Jeff Hays down the barrel of his own revolver. Her eyes were hard and filled with anger. Finally, she turned to Lassiter.

"I don't want this man to ever touch me again," she said.

"He won't," Lassiter promised. "Just give me the gun. Everything is fine."

Lassiter walked over and took the pistol from Lorna. She turned and cried against his chest as Will Carlson and Jake Broden, along with a number of other men, burst into the little clearing beside the river.

"What's all the shooting?" Carlson asked.

"Lorna just saved your horses from the Hays Gang," Lassiter told him, motioning toward the five horses, including the roan, grazing nearby.

"I only saw Jeff Hays," Carlson said, looking down at the wounded outlaw. "You mean the whole gang was out here?"

"There were only two other men that I saw," Lassiter told him, "but there might have been more."

"I saw two others, besides Hays," Jake agreed. "I didn't see no more of them around."

"I think there was only the three of them," Lorna said, drying her eyes. "The other two rode away."

"They likely wanted your roan, Will," Jake speculated. "They didn't want to make a big show, so they just sent three of them. They didn't figure Lorna was going to be here. They musta mistook her for Lanna."

Jeff Hays was staring at Lorna, a confused expression on his face.

"That's right," Lassiter told him. "You've got the wrong woman. This is Lanna's twin sister from Kansas City."

Hays squinted. "I don't believe that."

"Well, we've got ourselves a prize, don't we?" Carlson said, walking over to where Hays was holding his knee, still staring at Lorna. "You ain't too smart, are you?"

"You ain't about to do nothing to me," Hays spat back. He turned to look at Lorna. "That woman belongs to my brother. I just come to get what's rightfully ours."

"Didn't you hear what this man just said?" Carlson pointed to Lassiter. "This woman isn't who you think she is."

"She's who I think she is, all right," Hays argued. "And she belongs to us."

"What about those horses you're holding over there?" Carlson asked. "Are they rightfully yours?"

"I don't know nothing about the horses," Jeff said. "I want that woman. She belongs to my brother."

"I don't belong to your brother," Lorna corrected him angrily. "And Lanna doesn't belong to your brother, either."

"Lanna never said she had no twin," Jeff said. "I still don't believe you."

"It doesn't matter," Lassiter told Hays. "You're in no position to be demanding anything right now. You'd be a lot better off to just keep your mouth shut."

"He's soon going to have his mouth permanently closed," Carlson said. He walked over and picked up the rope. He held it in front of Jeff. "I think maybe we can use this to stretch your neck. There's a nice big cottonwood on the edge of town where everyone can watch. What do you think about that?"

Lassiter watched Jeff's face turn chalk white. Even though he was suffering intense pain in his ruined knee, the outlaw was distracted by the death threat. He finally gathered enough courage to try to make Carlson change his mind about hanging him. He brought up his gun-happy brother. "You'd be smart to just let me ride out of here," Jeff said, "unless you want my brother Carson down on you."

"Even if you could ride, we wouldn't let you go," Carlson said with a laugh. "You made yourself available, and we're going to take advantage of it."

"My brother will come here and wipe you all out," Jeff threatened.

"I'm not real worried about your brother," Carlson said. "I've been getting some of the ranchers together and soon your kind will be long gone. There are three men who have located your hideout. Your brothers are going to end up just like you, with their necks stretched at the end of a rope."

Carlson then left to claim his roan stallion and join the other men in their discussion about hanging Jeff Hays. Lorna stood beside Lassiter and stared at the young outlaw.

"They will hang him, won't they?" Lorna said. "They're really going to do it."

"What made you think they wouldn't?" Lassiter asked her.

"I just didn't think they would really hang a man."

"You just about shot him to death," Lassiter pointed out. "What's the difference?"

"I guess there isn't any," Lorna agreed.

Lassiter watched Jeff Hays, whose eyes were even wilder now. He was looking around desperately for a way out, but there were too many men around him. He hadn't scared Carlson and had, in fact, given Carlson more incentive to go ahead and organize his stranglers against the whole gang. There seemed to be no hope.

Lorna took Lassiter aside. "How long will it be until they hang him?"

"Soon. Why?"

"If he thought I was Lanna, then maybe we can learn more about her from him. Do you think that's possible?"

"He's not long for this world," Lassiter told her. "Besides, I don't know what he could tell us. Or what he *would* tell us, for that matter. We've got the map of Arrow Creek. That's enough."

"I somehow feel he knew her real well," Lorna said. "I don't know why, I just feel that way." Lorna put her hands over her face as though she was going to cry.

Lassiter held her. She was trembling. There were no tears, but he saw that her face was lined with worry as she looked up at him.

"Would you please ask that man about my sister?"

"I'll ask him whatever you want," Lassiter told her. "But don't think for a minute he's going to say anything. He doesn't appear to be in much of a mood for conversation."

"I would just like to know how long ago Lanna left

Carson Hays and a few things about her," Lorna said. "She is my twin sister. I'd like to understand her more."

"I'll do what I can," said Lassiter. He left Lorna in the shade of a tree and returned to Jeff Hays.

"What do you want now?" Hays asked. "You people had better let me go."

"I need to know some things about Lanna Hays," Lassiter told him. "How long ago did Lanna leave your brother?"

Hays motioned over to where Lorna was standing. "You and her are pulling some trick here. I don't know what it is, but you're both crazy. She's right over there." Hays was shaking his head. His face held a strange smile, like his mind was starting to reach the breaking point. "I don't know what you think you're doing by trying to kid me about this twin sister story, but I know Lanna, and that's her." He pointed to Lorna again.

"Lorna needs help in finding Lanna," Lassiter told him. "Believe me, that is not Lanna."

Hays shook his head. He rocked in pain as he held his shattered knee.

"Well, if you don't want to give us any idea about when Lanna left, what she was like, or what her habits were, then I guess we'll just watch you hang," Lassiter said.

"They won't hang me," Jeff said with conviction. "They wouldn't dare, not with my brother Carson back in the country."

"I don't think you understand," Lassiter said slowly. "They intend to hang you and the rest of your gang. To the last man. Didn't you hear Will Carlson say that?"

Jeff stopped shaking his head. Lassiter pointed over to where the men were gathering. One of them was building a noose on the end of the rope Carlson had picked up.

"They're not getting ready for a picnic," Lassiter pointed out.

Jeff's eyes widened. He began to get scared again. He had tried to tell himself that Carlson and the others were too afraid of his brother to hang him and suffer the consequences. Now he realized that Will Carlson was too angry to be afraid of anybody.

"They're going to hang me?" he asked, his voice cracking.

Lassiter nodded. "If you want to see Lanna get out of this country and away from trouble, you'll tell me as much as you can about her. We need to find her."

Jeff lowered his head and laughed. Jake Broden came over and took Lassiter aside. Jake said he had been talking with some of the men who had nearly lost their horses to Jeff Hays and the other two outlaws. They wanted to hang Jeff immediately. "I don't know if it's a very good idea," Jake told Lassiter. "I don't want to be involved in no strangler hangings. He should just go to jail and stand trial."

"You're probably right about that," Lassiter agreed, "but you seem to be in the minority around here."

"Why don't they just hold him and have a territorial marshal come get him?" Jake asked.

"Carlson knows it would be hard to get a conviction against him," Lassiter said. "There would be no proof he had ever stolen any horses, since the horses never left here. He would be out and back with his brothers before long."

Jake shrugged. "That could be," he said with a nod and a tug on his suspenders. "But hanging a man right off like this can be a mistake. Maybe they could hold him here and draw his brothers in."

"His brothers will come whether they hang him or

not,'' Lassiter said. ''But you're right, they should take all of them to jail and have them stand trial.''

''Maybe you should tell them that,'' Jake suggested.

''I'm the last person they would listen to,'' Lassiter said. ''Carlson thinks I'm an outlaw myself. It's even possible he thinks I'm part of the Hays Gang.''

Jake's eyes widened. ''Why would he think that?''

''Carlson doesn't trust anybody,'' Lassiter explained. ''I've got two guns, and I can use them. That's reason enough for him.''

''Yes, but you're helping Lorna. Can't he see that?'' He turned to point to Lorna, but she wasn't there. Lassiter looked around and saw that she was standing near Jeff Hays, talking to him. She saw Lassiter and Jake watching them and hurried over.

''He still thinks I'm Lanna,'' Lorna told Lassiter. ''He won't believe otherwise. So now he's saying things about his brother. Now that he's going to die, he says that he wishes he had stood up to Carson. He always wanted to take me away from the stealing and the killing, but he just couldn't bring himself to do it.''

Lassiter and Jake both stared at Lorna. ''Jeff Hays told you he never did want to be involved in the stealing and killing, and wanted to take Lanna away from it?''

''Yes.''

Lassiter looked back to Jake. ''If Jeff Hays will tell his story in court, then these ranchers have a case against the Hays Gang. They shouldn't hang Jeff Hays.''

Lassiter led Lorna and Jake over to where Will Carlson and the other men were throwing the rope over the limb of the big cottonwood. Lassiter told Carlson and the others that it would be better if they allowed Jeff Hays to live so that he could testify in court against his two brothers and the rest of the gang.

"It would be a lot better that way," Jake said earnestly. "It would be all legal."

"We haven't got time for courts," Carlson insisted. "No more thieving."

"How many of you men have lost horses to the Hays Gang?" Lassiter asked them.

"We just about lost five," Carlson broke in.

"But you haven't lost any yet," Lassiter pointed out. "If you hang Jeff Hays and the territorial marshal comes to ask questions, how are you going to answer them?"

Carlson looked to the other men and back to Lassiter. "I don't think *we* have to worry about answering any questions," he told Lassiter. "We've got a right to protect what's ours."

Carlson pushed his way past Lassiter and Jake, followed by the other men. More people had congregated near the tree, awaiting the hanging.

Jake Broden shook his head and turned to Lassiter. "I don't want to be a part of this," he said. "I'm taking my wagons and heading back to Fort Benton."

Jake left and Lassiter moved Lorna back out of the way. By now, everyone had arrived from the celebration to witness the hanging. Carlson and the other men hauled Hays to his horse, beneath the cottonwood. Everyone was still while they forced him up into the saddle.

"Let this be a warning to all horse thieves," Carlson announced to the people. "This man will die today for his crimes, and others like him will pay the same way."

"I've got a piece of paper," one of the men said to Hays. "Anything you want to write to somebody? You haven't got a lot of time."

"I don't need to write nothing," Jeff told the man. "It's you people who'd better do the writing. There won't be a one of you left alive when my brothers hear of this."

Carlson slapped Jeff's horse on the rump, and the horse bolted forward. Lorna and many of the onlookers gasped while Jeff Hays kicked and jerked until the rope finally strangled the last currents of life out of him.

Lorna turned away, facing the river. "I want to find my sister as soon as possible and get out of this country," she said. "People die too quickly around here."

8

WALLER AND GRUBER reached the hideout to find Lonnie and the rest of the gang saddling their horses. Waller was plenty scared. He didn't know how he was going to break the news about Jeff to Lonnie. He knew things would just get worse when Carson got back.

Waller knew how badly Lonnie wanted the roan stallion for Carson. He didn't know whether Lonnie would be madder over losing his brother or the horse.

"Where's the roan?" Lonnie Hays asked Waller as he and Gruber rode up. "Where's Jeff?"

"Jeff got himself shot by Lanna," Waller replied. "Me and Gruber had to ride out. There wasn't nothing we could do."

"*What?*" Lonnie said with disbelief. "Jeff got shot by Lanna?"

"Shot in the leg," Waller said. "But he ain't dead yet, not that we know of."

"Lanna?" Lonnie said again. "I thought she was hid out somewhere. She was there in Rocky Point?"

"Plain as day," Waller answered. "She was dressed up like some lady from the city or something."

"Lanna dressed up?" Lonnie Hays grew confused. "What was she doing in Rocky Point?"

"We just saw her there with some big stranger dressed in black," Gruber said. "He wore two big guns."

"Lanna's got herself another man," Lonnie commented. "Carson won't like to hear that, not at all. He'll kill him for sure."

Lonnie thought about how Jeff had some kind of crazy notion that Lanna cared about him. Jeff likely got beside himself with anger when he saw Lanna with another man. But getting himself shot only complicated their many problems. Carson would go crazy when he got back.

"I wish you two would have brought him back here, with that roan." Lonnie slapped his pant leg. "There's going to be more than hell to pay when Carson gets back."

Waller and Gruber looked at one another.

"When's Carson supposed to be back?" Waller wanted to know.

"In a few days or so," Lonnie answered. "Jeff should be with us when he gets here, that's for certain. Why the hell did you leave him there?"

"I told you," Waller said. "We'd have gotten ourselves shot."

"The whole town was coming," Gruber said, beginning to wonder what Lonnie was going to do with them. "And that woman was waving Jeff's pistol around like she was crazy."

"You know how Lanna can shoot," Waller said. "You know how she handles a gun. She could have killed us both."

"So you ran from a woman like rabbits," Lonnie said

angrily. "You just high-tailed it like a couple of yellow-bellied skunks."

"You should have been there!" Waller said angrily. "You could have seen for yourself!"

"You don't tell me what I should and shouldn't do," Lonnie Hays spat, pointing his finger at Waller. "You'd just better watch yourself. We better get Jeff back before Carson returns."

"Just how do you plan to get him back?" Waller asked.

"We'll ride in there now and get him," Lonnie said. "That's what we'll do. You and Gruber can lead the way, and you'd better not ride out on us when the shooting starts."

As Jeff Hays's body turned in slow circles beneath the cottonwood bough, the last of the crowd moved away from the scene. The festivities were winding down, and the hanging had been sobering.

Lassiter watched with Lorna while the men and women from the steamboat prepared to board. The boat would depart shortly and most of its passengers were eager to get on. The rumor that the Hays Gang would return for revenge was enough to make them want to be off as soon as possible.

"We've got to get a horse for you," Lassiter told Lorna as they approached his stallion. "As it is, it's going to be late when we get started."

Lorna pointed over to a group of men who were talking. "Didn't Will Carlson say we could buy a horse from him?" she asked.

Lassiter nodded. "But it looks like we're going to have to put it off again for a while." He pulled his Winchester from its scabbard and levered a bullet into the barrel.

"What are you doing?" Lorna asked.

Lassiter pointed to the edge of town, where a group of riders was approaching in a cloud of dust.

"The Hays Gang," Lassiter said. "They didn't waste any time getting back here, did they?"

People were already scattering for cover. Will Carlson and some of the men hurried over to Lassiter.

"There may be no need to fight them," Lassiter said. "They likely have come for Jeff Hays. Once they see his condition, they'll likely want to just leave town."

"What do you mean, 'no need to fight them'?" Carlson asked, with an edge to his voice. "They're coming right into town as bold as you please. We'd have them in our gunsights, easy."

Lassiter turned to Carlson. "You mean you'd just open fire on them? Shoot a bunch of men in cold blood?"

"They're horse thieves."

"They're entitled to the benefit of the doubt," Lassiter pointed out. "Besides, you don't want to start a lot of gunplay with women and children around."

Carlson couldn't argue with Lassiter on that point. He scowled as he went into the saloon with Lorna and the other men. He was allowing Lassiter to talk for the group.

"If they open fire on you, you'll wish that you'd let me have my way," Carlson told Lassiter.

"If they open fire, then shoot all you want," Lassiter said. "But make them start it."

The gang, Lonnie Hays in front, rode boldly into Rocky Point. Lassiter met them in the middle of the street, cradling his rifle across his chest.

Lassiter could see the older outlaw with the thin lips pointing to him and talking to the others as they pulled their horses up a short ways from Lassiter's position.

"I'm Lonnie Hays," the outlaw told Lassiter. "Where's my brother Jeff?"

"You'll find him at the edge of town," Lassiter informed him, pointing to the big cottonwood that stood alone. "Did you bring a shovel?"

Hays looked over to the cottonwood and saw the form of his brother, limply hanging at the end of the rope. Hays stared across the distance in shock. The other outlaws with him were equally stunned. Finally, Hays recovered and his face twisted in anger.

"What the hell?" he asked Lassiter. "You lynched my brother? You people did that?"

Some of Hays's men began moving restlessly in their saddles. Lassiter could see some of them looking at one another, thinking about going for their guns.

"Keep your hands away from those guns," Lassiter warned.

None of the outlaws wanted to act alone. Lonnie Hays stared at the form of his brother in the distance.

"What did you hang him for?" Hays finally asked Lassiter.

"He was trying to steal horses," Lassiter said. "You know what happens to horse thieves."

Hays turned to Waller. "I thought you said he was just shot in the leg."

Waller shrugged. "He was. When we left, he was alive."

"You had no call to hang him," Hays told Lassiter. "Damn! You people are going to pay for this."

"It's time you shut down your operation around here," Lassiter told Hays. "That is, if you don't want to find yourself and the rest of your bunch in your brother's condition."

"You talk pretty big for just one man," Hays said.

"One is enough," Lassiter pointed out. "You don't want to die, and I doubt if the rest of your men do either. Certainly not those two who rode out on your brother."

Lonnie Hays turned and scowled at Waller and Gruber. His face was red, and he clenched his fists tightly.

Lassiter knew the diversion had worked. By turning Lonnie Hays's anger toward two of his own men, he had effectively nullified any intention Hays might have of starting a shootout. Hays was now thinking that his brother would not be dead now if Waller and Gruber hadn't ridden out on him.

"Don't listen to him," Waller told Hays. "I say we shoot him."

"Come on up front and make your play," Lassiter challenged.

Waller looked to Lonnie Hays for support. "What do you say? Let's all pull at once."

"Go cut Jeff down," Hays told Waller and Gruber. "Get him on his horse and bring him over here."

"What about him?" Waller asked Lonnie Hays. He was hoping they would open fire on Lassiter and cut him down, even if some of them got shot in the process. It would take the heat off him and Gruber. "Let's shoot him."

"Go get Jeff!" Hays blared. "Now!"

Waller and Gruber kicked their horses into a gallop toward the edge of town and the big cottonwood. Hays and the others watched them in silence.

"Maybe your brother wouldn't have died if those two had stayed to help him," Lassiter added, solidifying his position. "There was just one woman who got the jump on them. And it wasn't even Lanna. From what I understand, Lanna would have killed all three of them."

Hays glared at Lassiter. "I don't know what you're talking about. I want to know now where Lanna is."

"Lanna's not here," Lassiter told him. "You and your brother both have trouble getting that through your heads. Her sister, Lorna, is the one who stopped your brother."

The outlaws all looked at one another and frowned at Lassiter.

"What do you mean, sister?" Hays finally asked Lassiter.

"Lanna has an identical twin sister. Her name is Lorna, and she's come looking for Lanna. She plans to take Lanna out of the badlands and back home with her. Your brother made a mistake and tried to kidnap Lorna. He lost out on everything."

"Why don't you just bring this woman out for us to see?" Lonnie Hays demanded.

Lassiter turned to the saloon and Lorna stepped out into the light. She stayed close to the doorway.

"Lanna's my sister," Lorna said. "My name is Lorna Jackson, and I live in Kansas City. I've come to find Lanna and take her back home with me."

Lonnie Hays stared. He did not understand what was happening. He concluded that this woman must be telling the truth. If she were Lanna, she wouldn't be here in town in the first place. Lanna, in a situation like this, certainly wouldn't be hiding in the saloon. She would be out in the street with the stranger, holding her own rifle.

Lorna turned and went back into the saloon. Hays turned back to his men, who were all silent.

Waller and Gruber returned with Jeff Hays's body draped over the saddle of his horse. Lonnie's wrath returned immediately. He cursed and slammed his fist against the pommel of his saddle. He could see where smears of blood had stained his brother's pants around the shattered knee.

"I can't believe Jeff's dead," one of the outlaws said in disbelief, staring at the body draped over the horse. "I just can't believe it."

Lonnie Hays was holding his hand to his brow, fighting the conflicting emotions of anger and grief that flooded through him. Again he cursed and turned to Lassiter.

"Was it this twin, Lorna, who shot my brother in the leg?"

Lassiter nodded. "She didn't have any choice."

"She shouldn't have shot him."

"It's too late for that," Lassiter told him. "It was your brother's decision to try to take her. Now that you know the whole story, it's time for you to ride out."

Lonnie Hays sat rigidly in the saddle. Lassiter detected a distinct change of attitude. Perhaps Hays was again considering a gunfight.

"Time to ride out," Lassiter repeated.

"You think you can order us around just like that?" Hays asked.

Lassiter nodded. "We've been through all this before. Either make your play or get out of town."

"I don't know who you are," Hays said, "but you've made a big mistake coming here. You won't leave this country alive."

"You'd better take your men out of here," Lassiter told Hays, "or you won't be around to see what happens to me."

Lonnie Hays turned to his men. "We'll just let it pass this time. This ain't over yet, not by a long shot." Hays turned back to Lassiter. "There's something you should know. I've got a brother named Carson Hays. Ever hear of him?"

Lassiter nodded casually. "I've heard the name."

"He'll be looking you up before long," Hays promised. "And when he does, you're a dead man."

"If he wants to see me, he'd better get a move on," Lassiter told Hays. "Much as I'd like to meet him, I don't have a lot of time to hang around here."

"Don't worry about that, mister," Hays said, turning his horse to leave. "Wherever you are, he'll find you."

9

WILL CARLSON CAME OUT of the saloon with Lorna and the other men. "I couldn't hear much of what was said," he told Lassiter. "How did you manage to keep from getting shot?"

"I told you," Lassiter explained. "Lonnie Hays knew if gunplay started, he'd be the first one with a bullet through his middle. He'd rather have his big brother do the hard work."

"You do have a way about you, don't you, Mr. Lassiter?" Carlson said. He turned to Lorna and smiled. "I owe you an awful lot, Mrs. Jackson. If it hadn't been for you, Jeff Hays and those other two would have my stallion somewhere out in those badlands now. There's no way I would have ever seen him again."

"Well, don't thank me," Lorna said. "That man was trying to take me, and I just got mad enough to grab his pistol. But I'm still having a difficult time with the way he died."

"I'm sorry about that, ma'am," Carlson said. "What I

wanted to tell you was that I'd like to show my gratitude by offering you one of my other horses. I understand you will be riding a good distance, and you'll need a good, stout horse to carry you.''

"That's very generous of you, Mr. Carlson," Lorna said, "but I just couldn't.''

"Yes, you could," Carlson said, laughing. "I insist. I want you and Mr. Lassiter to ride out to my place with me, and you can pick the one you want from my herd. You can spend the night and leave to look for your sister in the morning. I'm sure I can borrow a horse for you to get out to my ranch.''

Lorna smiled. "You're very kind, Mr. Carlson. I certainly appreciate your generosity.''

Carlson spoke with the other men for a time, while Lassiter and Lorna watched from beside Lassiter's stallion. The men talked and nodded, looking over at Lassiter often. Carlson finally returned, leading a small black pinto mare.

He looked to Lassiter. "What do you say we get going before it gets any later?''

Will Carlson's ranch was nothing more than a cabin and a large log barn used for storing tack and caring for horses. He didn't run cattle on the open range like most of the other livestock producers. He ran a horse ranch.

"That's why I'm so vulnerable to men like the Hays boys," Carlson explained to Lorna and Lassiter as they dismounted and made their way inside his cabin. "I have a lot of horses that I sell to neighboring ranchers for use mainly during roundup in the spring. The rest of the year, I'm raising colts. Stock thieves get a lot more for a good horse than they ever could for a beef critter.''

It was obvious Carlson lived alone and had for some time. The cabin was littered with clothes and likely hadn't been dusted for some time. But the wood stove was clean, and the tin plates and cups were covered by a clean layer of cloth.

Carlson started coffee on the stove. It didn't matter to Lorna or Lassiter whether he had ever been married or why he was in the middle of the badlands by himself. He wanted to give Lorna a horse, and she was happy to oblige him.

Lassiter considered telling Carlson that they would just as soon start looking for Lorna's sister right away and not stay the night. Carlson was taking his time with the coffee, making small talk and looking for the coffee cups.

"I used to have some nice china cups around here," he said, rummaging through a box. "I guess tin will have to do."

"It will taste just as good to me," Lorna told him. "This is very nice of you, and I would like to thank you again."

"Think nothing of it," Carlson said. "You did me a real favor by saving my stallion."

Lassiter wanted to ask him to show Lorna the horses, but he couldn't bring himself to do it. He didn't think it courteous to rush Carlson, who was, after all, giving up good property. It was true, she had saved his stallion from the hands of the Hays gang, but it seemed overly generous to be rewarding her with the pick of his herd.

Carlson poured coffee and began discussing his view of the thief problem.

"There's only one way to do it," he was saying. "That's to wipe them out right away before they get too strong."

"How long have you known they were around here?" Lassiter asked him.

"Rumors have circulated over the past year," Carlson replied. "But no one nearby lost any horses. Everybody figured the gang stole them from other places. Then this happened today."

"What about Carson Hays?" Lassiter asked. "Do you know anything about him?"

"I've heard he's real dangerous," Carlson replied. "I've never seen the man, but I can say that he won't stand up to organized ranchers."

Lassiter looked hard at Carlson. "Organized ranchers" could mean only one thing: Carlson was talking about stranglers, and he had most likely put a plan together already with some of the local men to go after the Hays Gang.

"I was raised in the gold camps of Virginia City, so I've seen what can happen when a bunch of thieves get a foothold somewhere," Carlson rambled. "Ever hear of Henry Plummer? He was dangerous, but he didn't last. Carson Hays and his bunch won't last, either. All of them will go, *all* of them!"

"It doesn't appear to me that you folks around here are going to let things get out of hand," Lassiter told Carlson.

"You can bet on that," Carlson said with a nod. He poured more coffee for everyone, then sat down and sipped nervously from his cup. "We aren't going to tolerate anything like those road agents got away with when I was a kid. It took the people a long time before they finally came to their senses and strung those guys up."

"You saw all that as a child?" Lorna asked him.

Carlson nodded, the muscles in his small face tightening. "I saw it all. I was just a schoolkid, but I learned a lot. Now I can spot a thief a long ways away."

Carlson related how his father had gone broke in the gold fields, and his mother had left them. When his father had gotten himself shot to death in a saloon brawl, young Will had migrated onto a ranch to break horses. He could stick with a bronc better than most. After three years there, he moved on to the badlands.

"Despite the problem with rustlers," he told them, "there's good money in horses. Ranchers and the military both need good horses all the time." He turned to Lorna. "So what's this I hear about your sister being an outlaw? And a *twin* sister to boot."

Lorna blushed. "It's true. Lanna is my twin sister. But I don't know about the part of her being an outlaw."

"I know that she is," Carlson said. "I hope we don't have to hang her." He looked hard at Lassiter. "You're looking for her, is that it?"

"The fact is," Lassiter told Carlson evenly, "Lorna hasn't see her sister since they were separated as little girls. And since Lanna is now in hiding from Carson Hays, that would suggest she doesn't agree with his line of work."

"Well, you've got a point," Carlson agreed. He got up and moved toward the coffeepot. "But I'm still not sure, after all of this, that you two aren't cut from the same bolt of cloth as the Hays boys, maybe just decorated a whole lot fancier."

"You think my sister is an outlaw, and that *I'm* an outlaw as well?" Lorna asked.

Lassiter was used to various insults of that nature, but Lorna was offended. Carlson just stood near the stove, leaning against the door frame.

"Mr. Carlson, do you really think I staged that whole thing with that outlaw?" Lorna continued. "Would I shoot him in the leg like that if I was part of their gang?"

"Could have been an accident," Carlson suggested. "Nobody else saw it. Maybe you were getting ready to leave with them when he shot himself in the leg. That's happened before. Maybe you *are* Lanna Hays and there is no twin sister."

"Did you ask us to come all the way out here so you could share this nonsense with us?" Lassiter asked him. "If that's the case, we've wasted a lot of time."

There was the distinct sound of trampling hooves coming into the ranch yard, and Lassiter stood up. Carlson grabbed a rifle from behind the stove and cocked the hammer.

"Just sit back down, Mr. Lassiter, or whatever your name is," Carlson ordered. "Put your hands on the table, and don't move them. I'll shoot you, I really will."

"There's no need to get excited," Lassiter told him. "I don't intend to force you to use that rifle."

"Now you're thinking smart," Carlson said, watching Lassiter sit down. "Just don't change your mind."

"What is this all about?" Lorna asked.

"We just don't know about you two yet, that's all," Carlson said. "We don't want to take any chances. You're not going anywhere until we get the rest of the Hays Gang."

Lassiter now realized that Carlson had been stalling so that the riders dismounting in front of the cabin could catch up. The "we" he was speaking of were the men he had talked to just before offering Lorna a free horse. The other men had waited just long enough to follow behind without being seen.

"So this was all a setup, wasn't it?" Lorna said to Carlson. "You told me you would give me a horse just to get us out here and hold us."

"Do you think you would have allowed us to hold you and Mr. Lassiter any other way?" Carlson asked.

"You're no better than the man you hanged today," Lorna said with contempt.

Carlson ignored Lorna and kept the rifle trained on Lassiter. He knew what Lassiter could do and wasn't about to make himself vulnerable in any way.

"This is a mistake," Lassiter said. "I'm not one of the Hays Gang, and Lorna *is* Lanna's twin sister."

"Maybe. Maybe not." Carlson's eyes were getting wider. He wished the men outside would hurry and come in.

"What you don't seem to realize, Mr. Carlson," Lorna then said, "is that Mr. Lassiter has gotten rid of a lot of the gang already. They know who he is and want him dead. How could he be a part of a gang that's after him?"

"That's all talk," Carlson said. "There's no proof that this man killed any of the gang. Just your word that he did."

"You saw what he did at Rocky Point today," Lorna then said. "How could you possibly think he's part of the gang?"

"He handled things pretty well in front of the saloon," Carlson agreed. "Too well, for my way of thinking. That's what made me wonder."

"You don't seem to understand, do you?" Lassiter said to Carlson.

"I think I do," Carlson said.

Five men then entered the cabin and looked hard at Lorna and Lassiter. They were led by a big rancher with a prominent jawbone, whom Lassiter recognized from among the men at the hanging of Jeff Hays.

Lassiter recognized all of them with the exception of a

middle-aged man with a red beard, who was apparently seeing Lorna for the first time.

"That's the woman, all right," he said emphatically. "She's the one."

"The one who did what?" Lassiter asked him.

"She was with Carson Hays when he and his bunch stopped my freight wagon just out of Helena last fall. I've driven freight over the Carroll Trail for a good while, and I never saw nothing like it. She damned near shot me."

"You're sure it was *this* woman?" Lassiter asked him.

"Positive."

"Is this the kind of clothing she was wearing when she was with Hays?" Lassiter asked.

"No," the man answered. "She had on pants and wore a gun. But that don't mean nothing."

"This woman has never worn pants in her life," Lassiter said.

The man scratched his red beard. "She's a spittin' image of that woman, I swear."

"Did you ever hear of identical twins?" Lassiter asked.

"What's he talking about?" the red-bearded one asked Carlson. "That outlaw woman has a twin sister?"

"And that's her right in front of you," Lassiter told the man. "She's no outlaw, you can see that."

"You believe him?" the big rancher asked Carlson.

"Of course not," Carlson replied. "That's what he's been trying to make everybody believe. He says this woman is a identical twin sister to Carson Hays's wife, and that she's up here from Kansas City to find Hays's wife and take her back."

Lassiter produced the picture of Lorna and her husband. "The woman is Lorna," Lassiter explained as the men passed the picture around. "You can certainly tell her husband is not Carson Hays. He's a man named Darren

Jackson, a federal judge down in Kansas City. He would be real upset if he knew what was happening here.''

The men all studied Lorna in silence. The red-bearded one was still scratching his head. The big one studied the picture and handed it back to Lassiter.

"Who are you, then?" he asked.

Lassiter once more related his story of coming up from Denver to help out a friend, who was looking for Lorna. It appeared to Lassiter as he told the story that half of the men wanted to believe him and half didn't. They began talking again.

"We don't know that any of what this man says is true," Carlson finally said. "I want to hold them both here until we get the rest of the gang. That way, if they are part of the bunch, they can't help them. If it turns out they're telling the truth, then there's nothing hurt."

"Only that you're keeping us from finding Lorna's twin sister," Lassiter protested.

"We can't help that," Carlson argued. "It's not smart to take any chances with you. So you and the lady will just have to make yourselves understand that."

Lassiter and Lorna were ushered out to Carlson's barn. The sun was nearly down, and the late light covered the badlands with gold. The men were now arguing among themselves about holding Lassiter and Lorna. Some of them didn't want to have to worry about the wrath of a federal judge. One in particular, the red-bearded one from Helena, had decided not to stay with the stranglers.

Lassiter again tried to talk sense into Carlson and the other men. The red-bearded driver was going back to Helena with his freight outfit, and Lassiter wanted the others to leave Carlson's idea alone as well. But no one else wanted to listen.

"If what you're saying is true," Carlson told him, "you

and the lady will be free soon enough. We're going to join up with some other men and go after the gang tonight.''

"One of their main members is missing," Lassiter informed them. "Carson Hays is off somewhere with part of the gang. He's the leader, and if you miss him, you'll lose the war against the Hays boys.''

"So how do you know all this, mister?" the big man asked Lassiter.

"I learned it from two members of the gang," Lassiter said. "A young outlaw who's now in jail in Fort Benton and Jeff Hays himself.''

"Or maybe you're just trying to throw us off," Carlson put in.

"If I was part of the gang," Lassiter said, "I wouldn't be telling you a damn thing. You ought to realize that.''

"Time will tell," Carlson told Lassiter.

"You men are biting off more than you can chew," Lassiter tried to warn them for the last time. "You should have listened to Jake Broden. He tried to talk you out of this strangler business. Or do you think he's also an outlaw?''

'We don't have to listen to you or Jake Broden,'' Carlson said. He looked to the big rancher and the other men. "Tie them up.''

Lassiter found himself being pushed down into a sitting position and bound securely to one of the main supports with a length of rope, while Lorna was tied to another log support just as tightly. When they had finished, the men left the barn, and Lassiter could hear them riding out of the yard.

"Carlson tricked us," Lorna said. "I should have known a free horse was too good to be true.''

"Carlson doesn't seem to care much about anything except getting the Hays Gang," Lassiter said. "He's not thinking too rationally, and he's got those other men following him.''

"So what happens now?" Lorna asked. "They just left us here without food or water.''

"Let's just hope Carlson can do the job he wants to do," Lassiter said. "Otherwise, we might be here for a long time.''

10

LONNIE HAYS was lying in his bunk, his eyes on the ceiling. The air was stifling and still. Sweat drenched his clothing while he watched the shadow movement of tree branches cast by moonlight through the open window over the bed.

It had been dark for some time and the day's events a thing of the past. But Lonnie Hays didn't want to feel the here and now. He didn't want things to be as they really were. Though he wished it were but a bad dream, his thoughts continually went back to just before twilight, when he had thrown the last shovelful of earth onto Jeff's grave.

He was reviewing everything in his mind, over and over again. What could he have done different? How could he have kept all this from happening? Jeff was dead, and he tried to think how he could have prevented it.

If he had only done one simple thing: left Jeff to guard the hideout and fetched the roan stallion himself. That, he concluded, would have prevented all of this. They would have the stallion now, and Jeff would be alive.

"Have that stallion for me when I get back," was all Lonnie could hear in his mind now. "I want that stallion!" Carson's demands were always uppermost in everyone's mind. But now that Jeff had died for those demands, everything was muddled.

Carson's wants took up everyone's time, and now they were becoming ever more unbearable. Carson wanted horses stolen and delivered, and he wanted the roan stallion, and he wanted Lanna back. Any one of those three was a tall order, but everything all at once was more than possible.

Nothing had gone right lately. The four who went to Fort Benton for supplies should certainly have been back way before Carson showed up with the horses and the rest of the gang. It didn't made sense.

And he was still puzzled by the woman who claimed to be Lanna's twin sister. That was the biggest twister of this whole thing. There was no doubt that she looked exactly like Lanna; but why hadn't Lanna mentioned she had a sister? No one had ever heard her mention anything about her family.

In addition, there was one man now who had brought himself firmly into the situation. Hays clenched his teeth and thought again about this stranger. No one had seen him before, and there was no way to understand how he had come into their country and what he was doing in the middle of all this. Whoever he was, he would soon wish he'd never seen Rocky Point.

Lonnie's thoughts wandered back to the incident that had cost his brother his life. He went over the way Waller and Gruber had described it and wondered now what he should do with the two men, and how much blame he should put on them for all this. Lonnie knew Jeff was impulsive and had likely gotten excited at seeing this woman who was Lanna's twin.

There was no excuse, though, for having gotten himself into a position to be shot, and then hanged by the angry ranchers.

Lonnie tried to decide what he would do now. Should he take Waller and Gruber and some of the men and go after that stranger and take the woman who claimed to be Lanna's sister? Or should he wait until Carson got back? Carson would certainly provide the strength it would take to stand up to the stranger. But how long would it take him to get back from Fort Benton with the four men who had gone in for supplies? If he was looking for Lanna, he might even send the men ahead and be gone for some time.

There was also the problem of going off and leaving the hideout guarded by too few men. More than ever now, the place needed defending until they could find a suitable new location. The three men who had discovered them could return at any time, and they would likely bring a host of stranglers with them. There were too many horses at stake here, too much of Carson's wrath to have to look forward to if something else happened.

The problems seemed insurmountable, especially in the strange and mournful haze of feelings left with Jeff's death. Lonnie couldn't help but shake his head time and time again. It didn't seem possible that his brother was gone, that he wasn't standing around talking about something he wanted to do, or daydreaming about Lanna. It was going to take some getting used to.

The more Lonnie thought about Jeff sealed forever in a grave, the angrier he got. It was enough that the ranchers had decided to organize a vigilante group, but this stranger making his bold appearance was intolerable. Backing everyone down by standing alone in the middle of the street was hard to imagine. Nobody did that to the Hays boys.

Lonnie still kicked himself for not opening fire against the stranger, even though the stranger was obviously good with a gun and knew what he was doing. Some of the men, including himself, might have taken a bullet; but at least when Carson got back he would know they had fought for the family honor.

Suddenly Lonnie heard yelling outside and his eyes blinked. He returned to the here and now and had twisted himself quickly to a sitting position when the door flew open. Gruber was framed by moonlight in the doorway.

"Somebody's coming," he told Lonnie. "A bunch of riders up on the trail above."

Hays leapt to his feet and grabbed a rifle from a deerhorn rack along the wall. "Get the boys together out front," he ordered. "Hurry!"

Lonnie rushed to where his horse was picketed and tightened down the saddle cinch. He thought for a moment and looked back to the two cabins, sitting with the lantern light filling them in the hot summer night. He realized if he worked this right, he wouldn't have to put himself or any of the men in jeopardy. He nodded to himself and calmly led his horse to a small corral and fastened the reins to a pole.

The other members of the gang came out of the other cabin, checking rifles and pistols. They gathered around Lonnie.

"Gruber says we've got company," Lonnie began. "I've got a plan that's going to work."

"Hadn't we better get on our horses and be ready to meet them when they get down here?" Waller asked.

"No, just listen to me," Lonnie told him. "I want you and Gruber to go back into the cabins and turn the lanterns down real low. Then I want all of you to tie your horses over here with mine, so that it looks like we're all in the cabins. I'll take you and Gruber with me up on the east hill. The rest of you get over on the other side above the cabins. If they're crazy enough to ride down here, wait until they're on the bottom, then move over and seal off the trail.''

''What if there's a lot of them?'' Gruber asked.

''It won't matter if there's a hundred of them,'' Lonnie told him. ''They'll be trapped in here and they won't know where to go. Just don't open fire until you see us shooting first. Got it?''

Everyone nodded and tied their horses with Lonnie's. They ran through the shadows and into position along the hill behind the cabins. Lonnie led Waller and Gruber to a small hollow filled with shadow set back from the front of the cabins.

''Here they come,'' Waller hissed, pointing up through the darkness.

On the trail at the top of the hill, a number of riders were silhouetted, getting ready to make their way down to the cabins.

''Don't get too anxious,'' Lonnie told Waller and Gruber. ''We want them close.''

Lonnie sat still in the darkness with Waller and Gruber, waiting patiently. He hoped the stranger was with the group. He should have stood up to that man before, but now he had his chance.

Will Carlson led the stranglers down the steep trail toward the outlaw hideout below. The shadows were dense along the hills above the bottom, but the moon was close to full and the light showed the cabins on the flat nestled up again the hillside.

There were a lot of horses grazing out in an open meadow, and some of the men exclaimed that they were certainly in the right place.

"I know right where we're at," Carlson said, stopping his horse to talk to the others. "I was out here the other day with two ranchers from the Judith Basin who wanted to buy horses from me. They'll be back as soon as we clean this nest of vermin out."

"They must be here," someone said. "There's a bunch of horses with saddles tied to that corral."

"They're likely getting ready for a midnight raid somewhere," Carlson speculated. "We caught them just right, holed up inside their cabins."

"How're we going to go about this?" another one of the men asked. "It almost seems too easy."

"We'll surround the cabins," Carlson said. "When everyone's in position, we'll tell them to come out. If they don't, we open up on them."

"We may have to burn them out," one of the men stated with anticipation.

"We'll do whatever we have to," Carlson said, nodding.

Everyone seemed content with the plan and Carlson led them the rest of the way down the hill. They surrounded the cabins and, with their rifles cocked, waited for a reply from within when Carlson demanded those inside come out with their hands in the air.

Suddenly there was gunfire from somewhere behind them; then from the hill along the trail above the cabins. Five men fell right away, including Will Carlson. The others tried to turn and ride out the way they had come, but were met with more gunfire. The shadows came alive with outlaws, and there was no way out for any of the stranglers. No one escaped.

*   *   *

Lonnie Hays yelled for everyone to hold their fire. He was relatively certain they had downed all the stranglers, and he didn't want any of his own men shooting one another by mistake. There was no need to take chances.

The night air was filled with the stench of spent powder. From here and there came moans through the darkness of wounded and dying men. The stranglers were scattered over the ground around the cabins. A few who had tried to escape were found along the trail away from the hideout. Most had been killed, but a few were found alive, including Will Carlson.

Lonnie knelt down next to Carlson, who was lying on his stomach, moaning. He turned Carlson over and looked down into his face.

"Want me to finish him?" Waller offered.

"No, hold off," Lonnie told him. "I want to find out some things from him first."

Hays took Carlson by the back of the shirt collar and dragged him into the doorway of the main cabin. Carlson had been shot through the lower back twice, both bullets going through to his stomach, then exiting out the front, one hole on each side of his navel.

Apparently neither bullet had struck an artery and the blood flow was minimal for the seriousness of the wounds. Carlson was almost totally conscious, but sinking deeper into shock. His wounds were mortal, but it was to be a slow, painful death.

"He's plugged real good, ain't he?" Gruber commented. "Wouldn't do no good to hang him now. He wouldn't even know what we were doing."

Lonnie Hays ignored the comments. He had other things on his mind. "Where's that stranger dressed in black?" he asked Carlson.

Carlson stared at Hays and belched uncontrollably. He vomited blood twice before Carlson got an answer out of him.

"You've got to get me to a doctor," Carlson begged. "Please, you've got to."

"Sure," Hays told him. "But I want some answers first."

"Then you'll get me to a doctor?"

"Sure. Where's that stranger?"

"You ain't taking me to—no doctor, are you? You're lying."

Hays laughed, as did the others now gathering to watch. It was particularly pleasing to Waller and Gruber.

"Where did that stranger go with the woman?" Hays then demanded. "Are they still in Rocky Point?"

Carlson turned away from Hays and closed his eyes, his face twisted in pain.

"I said, where's that stranger and the woman?" Hays demanded.

"Go—to hell," Carlson managed.

Lonnie looked into the cabin and then turned to Waller. "Go in there and bring me that jug of kerosene and one of them lanterns," he said. "This man don't want to talk to me, so I'll just cook him."

Carlson's eyes widened. He could hear the men talking among themselves, some laughing again, while Lonnie Hays looked down into his terrified face and made it plain things would be a lot better for him if he answered the questions.

"You—you wouldn't burn me, would you?" Carlson said.

"Did you hang my brother?" Hays asked.

Carlson's head fell back against the ground and he moaned.

"We'll see what happens," Hays said. "You answer my questions, and we'll see what happens."

"I want you to promise—promise you won't burn me," Carlson said. "Then I'll answer your questions."

Waller returned with the jug and a lantern. Carlson watched helplessly while Hays pulled the cork on the jug and tipped it over him. The smell of kerosene was strong as Hays drenched his clothes.

"What did you want me to promise?" Hays asked Carlson.

"Wait, just—wait," Carlson stammered. "I'll tell you where they are, just don't—"

"Where are they?" Hays demanded.

"They're—tied in my barn." Carlson struggled to get the words out. "I thought maybe the stranger was part of your gang, and that maybe the woman was lying. I thought she might be Lanna Hays."

"How about your roan stallion?" Hays asked. "Is the horse at your place?"

"The roan is in the corral beside the barn," Carlson said. "I answered you—I did—now can you get me to a doctor?"

"Sure," Hays said. He leaned over and took Carlson by the collar once again and hauled him back away from the cabin, as Carlson choked and coughed.

The other men followed and gathered around, anticipating something. Hays stood with the chimney off the lantern and lit a small stick into a miniature torch.

"No!" Carlson croaked. "No—don't!"

Hays flipped the burning stick onto Carlson's chest and his clothes burst into flames. He began to scream and jerk while Hays looked on solemnly and the other men laughed.

Lonnie Hays went back to the horses, thinking all the

while about getting Lassiter and the roan stallion. They would deal with the woman, whoever she was, at the same time.

Later, the gang rode in a column up the trail and out of the hideout. Will Carlson's remains smoldered in the moonlight.

11

A FAINT HINT of light colored the eastern sky when Lassiter came awake to the sounds of a horse. Lorna was already leaning forward against her bonds.

"Are they back already?" she asked hopefully.

"I doubt it. There's just one rider."

"Maybe it's Carlson come back to set us free," Lorna said. "Maybe they've found the rest of the Hays Gang and he knows now that you were telling the truth."

"It's too soon for that," Lassiter informed her. "Besides, I doubt if Carlson would come by himself, especially knowing what I think of him now."

"Then who do you think it is?" Lorna asked.

"I don't know, but I expect we'll find out soon enough."

The hoofbeats passed the barn and stopped in front of the cabin, assuring Lassiter that it couldn't be Carlson coming back to apologize. Before long, there was the sound of footsteps approaching the barn.

"Lassiter, you in there? Lorna?"

Lassiter recognized the voice of Jake Broden.

"I'm in here," Lassiter said. "Lorna and I are tied up."

Jake hurried into the barn and began freeing them. "I wasn't sure how I'd find you," he said.

"How did you know we were here?" Lorna asked.

"I ran into another freighter, a stranger with a red beard, at Clagett's Landing," Jake replied. "He was talking with Old Charlie about you and Lorna, and how Carlson thought you two were part of the Hays Gang. He'd seen you at Carlson's ranch. Carlson was holding a gun on you."

Lassiter nodded. Lorna turned to him, remembering the man with the red beard and how he had thought she was Lanna.

"Isn't he the one from Helena?" Lorna asked.

"That's him," Lassiter said. "Lucky for us he didn't want to go with Carlson after the Hays Gang."

"I asked him what Carlson was up to," Jake continued, "and he told me he was leading a bunch of stranglers after the Hays boys. I decided to borrow one of Charlie's horses and leave my wagon at the landing. I didn't know what I could do for you, or if it was too late, but I came as fast as I could."

"Lucky for us that you did," Lassiter said. "Carlson and the rest of them may get themselves killed. We would have been left here to rot."

Lassiter helped Lorna to her feet. They were both tired and sore, and it took some time for Lorna to ease her cramping muscles. Lassiter rubbed the stiffness from his wrists and arms while he listened to Jake.

"This strangler business has been coming on for some time," Jake was saying. "Will Carlson has gotten so he don't trust a single soul. On top of it, he wants to be some kind of general or something."

"I could see he was eager to take charge of things in Rocky Point," Lassiter said. "He doesn't know what he's getting into when he takes off after a bunch of killers."

Jake related that the red-bearded freighter from Helena had said further that Carlson wasn't going to stop until he had hanged all the thieves north of the Missouri. There were a lot of men combing the badlands to locate the Hays Gang hideout, and very few of them had ever gone out on the hunt for outlaws before.

"It's not like a roundup," Lassiter said, helping Lorna out of the barn and into the dawn light. "You don't just go out and herd thieves into a neat group so you can handle them. They've got ideas of their own."

"I told Carlson that when we talked about hanging Jeff Hays," Jake said. "I was running a freight wagon back and forth from Utah to the Virginia City gold camps when they went to Robber's Roost and strung those men up. Carlson was just a punk kid then, and he thought at the time there was nothing to it."

Lassiter led the way into the corrals. There were a number of horses penned up, including Carlson's roan stallion and Lassiter's stallion. It was apparent the two horses were getting ready to fight.

"That's not real smart, putting two stallions together like that," Jake observed. "I can't figure why Carlson didn't ride his horse after the gang."

"Too many cracks and holes to injure a horse in," Lassiter said. "Riding these badlands in the dark is not advisable under any circumstances."

Lorna surveyed the horses in the corral and gave her opinion of them. "There are some nice mares in there," she said. "I can understand why Carlson worries about thieves. He should hire some men to help him, though."

Lassiter found his saddle leaning against the outside of

the corral. "At least they didn't bother anything in my saddlebags," he said, looking at the map still neatly folded where he had last placed it.

"They were likely in too big a hurry," Jake speculated. "Carlson always wants to do what's on his mind right away, like there's no tomorrow."

"I wasn't sure what they were going to do with my stallion," Lassiter said, still surprised. "I heard a couple of them talking about using him to go after the Hays Gang."

"That makes them no better than the outlaws," Lorna said angrily.

"There's a fine line out here between who's bad and who's good," Jake pointed out. "Sometimes that line ain't there at all."

Lassiter saddled his stallion while Jake discussed the rustler problem and how he could see Carlson's point. The lack of authorized lawmen made it open season on horses and livestock for thieves and road agents. It was becoming increasingly difficult for ranchers to stay in business. It had gotten to the point where the ranchers had to do something to eliminate the problem.

"There's just one thing wrong with that," Lassiter told Jake as he finished tightening the latigo strap on the saddle. "When stranglers start hanging people, sometimes they hang a few innocent men in their eagerness to clean up."

"That's why I say you should lead them," Jake said.

"They're going to have to handle things on their own from here on out," Lassiter said. "After what's happened, I don't have much loyalty left for the bunch around here."

"I don't blame you," Jake said. "What do you plan to do now?"

"My only concern is to help Lorna find her sister and

get them off to Kansas City, where Lorna's husband lives,'' Lassiter replied. "We've wasted a lot of time and got ourselves in trouble for no good reason, and I've got a friend who's laid up in Fort Benton with two bullet holes in him. This bunch of outlaws has been a real sore spot for me.''

Jake grinned at Lassiter. "I think you're more of a sore spot for them, if the truth were known,'' he commented. "You've made them real short of men.''

"There's still enough of them left to cause a lot of problems,'' Lassiter said. "That's why we've got to find Lorna's sister and get out of this country.''

Lassiter climbed on his stallion and was leaning over to help Lorna on behind him when Jake pointed to the north and announced they had company.

"Could be Carlson and his bunch on their way back,'' Jake decided, "but I don't know for sure.''

Lassiter watched as the cloud of dust in the distance drew nearer. He suggested to Jake that they just ride on and not wait for the riders, whether they turned out to be Carlson and the stranglers or someone else.

"I don't want to have to listen to Carlson any more,'' Lassiter said. "And if it's anybody other than Carlson, we could find ourselves in a lot of danger.''

Jake frowned. "If it is somebody else, it would have to be the Hays Gang, wouldn't it?''

"That's likely,'' Lassiter told him.

Jake quickly climbed into the saddle. He was now thinking that Carlson and his stranglers might have gotten themselves into real trouble, or even gotten themselves killed. If this was the Hays Gang coming, they could count on a less than friendly exchange.

"Why don't we just let these other horses out of the corral?'' Jake then suggested. "That roan and the others will scatter and maybe take up some of Hays's time, if that's what he came here for.''

"You can bet if that's the Hays Gang coming, they want the horses," Lassiter said.

"And you, too," Jake said. "If they see you, they'll really want you and Lorna."

"It's time to leave," Lassiter said. "The better head start we get, the better off we'll be."

Lonnie Hays stopped his men at the top of a hill that overlooked Will Carlson's ranch, where the badlands smoothed out to a broad and open valley. Below, the corral near the barn was empty. The gate was open, and the horses that had been contained were now scattered over the bottom, including the roan stallion.

"What the hell is this?" Hays said, watching the horses running in every direction. "What happened here?"

"Looks like somebody just let them out," Gruber said. "They're still running like they just got freed."

Then Waller pointed along the valley bottom. "Riders out there, Lonnie, a good ways out."

Lonnie Hays squinted into the distance.

"Way out on the flat," Waller added, continuing to point. "They're a good ways out, but I can make them out. There's one riding alone, and two riding double on another horse. It looks like that stranger's red stallion to me, and like he's got that woman on behind him."

Lonnie stood up in the stirrups. "It looks as if you're right, Waller. I'll be damned."

Waller turned to Lonnie Hays and smiled. "We could catch them. That stranger's horse ain't going to hold up long running like that with two on his back."

Lonnie pointed to the horses and told three of the men to gather them and get them back into the corral. "The rest of you come with me," he said. "I'm going to get that stranger, just like I promised."

Jake turned in his saddle, yelling to Lassiter. "They're coming after us! They'll be on us in no time."

Lassiter realized that his stallion could ordinarily outrun most everything on four legs. But with Lorna on behind, it would only be a matter of time until the excess weight slowed them down enough for Hays and his outlaws to catch them. Their only chance was to find a suitable place to make a stand.

Lonnie Hays and his men were steadily gaining. Lassiter saw the outlaws splitting into two groups in an attempt to force them into a trap. If they could be herded between the two groups, there would be little or no chance to fight effectively.

Lassiter knew they would have to make certain they found a place where they could hold the outlaws off indefinitely. It couldn't be in open country. And the outlaws would be hard to stop; there were far too many of them to expect Hays to give up easily.

Lonnie Hays and the gang, spread out in a wide column coming along the flats, continued to gain on them. Lassiter knew the outlaws would be upon them soon and where they were, there would be no chance to defend. Their only chance was to slow the gang down somehow and maintain a good lead until they found a place to make a stand.

Lassiter made a decision that would at least give them a better chance of escape than they had now. He turned his stallion off the main trail and into the treacherous country up from the bottom. It would be a hard climb through a series of steep hills, and a rough test for his stallion; but if they could make it over the top and into the jumble of rugged land on the other side, they would be able to either get away or find a place to hold Hays off.

The move into the badlands slowed the Hays gang down, as Lassiter had hoped. The half that Hays was leading had to move into single file and climb the trails much more slowly than Lonnie would have liked. But now there was a new worry: the other group had taken a different trail and was somewhere nearby, trying to cut them off.

Lassiter knew he couldn't think about where the other half of the gang had gone. He had to concentrate on getting to cover. They were far better off now, for taking the chase into the steep country gave them the chance they needed to find a suitable location to settle in against the outlaws.

The country was filled with pockets and gullies to hide in, places no one could see into. But Lassiter didn't want to take the chance of being found; he wanted to face the opposition head-on.

Across a broad and open coulee, Lassiter spotted a thick stand of scrub pine along the top of a ridge. It was perfect. The vantage point was excellent, and there was a lot of cover to move around in. Hays and his gang would have to cross the steep and open hillside to get to them, a move that would cost Hays dearly if he was foolish enough to try.

As they started down the slope, Lassiter noticed the other half of the outlaws breaking over a ridge just to their right, riding at breakneck speed to cut them off. Lassiter knew that unless they stopped these outlaws, Hays and the other half of the gang would come over the top, and they would be surrounded.

12

LASSITER RODE HIS STALLION down the steep slope, gauging how far it was to the opposite side and up into the trees. It was going to be a tough ride, and they certainly wouldn't make it before the outlaws were well within rifle range.

The outlaws rode as fast as their horses could take them along a slope colored white in places from thick, chalky soil, which flew like talcum under the horses' hooves. Once they crossed a small cut along the slope, there would be no stopping them.

Lassiter reined in his stallion and pulled his rifle. "Lorna, get on behind Jake. Hurry!"

"What for?" Lorna asked. "We can make it to the trees, can't we?"

"No, my horse won't be able to make it up that opposite slope in time with both of us on," Lassiter told her. "They'll shoot us like ducks on a pond. Jake will ride with you on back toward the trees while I slow them down."

"By yourself? That's too dangerous," Jake insisted. "Let Lorna go on ahead. I'll stay back and help you."

"No!" Lassiter told him, pushing Lorna up behind him on his horse. "You take Lorna across. You'll do us a lot more good there. Once you get into the trees, you can shoot at them from that angle. If we all stay here, Hays will come over the ridge behind us and trap us. We won't have a chance."

"What if Hays comes over while you're here?" Lorna asked. "Then you're trapped by yourself."

"I'll be out of here and with you two by then," Lassiter said confidently. "Now get going."

Jake grumbled and kicked his horse into a run toward the bottom of the hill, while Lassiter leveled his rifle on the lead rider. Some of the outlaws stopped and began to shoot at Jake and Lorna, sending small puffs of dust up all around Jake's churning horse.

The lead outlaw continued toward Lassiter, and Lassiter fired. The outlaw tumbled backward from the horse and rolled down, covering himself in the chalky white earth. Lassiter levered in another round and shot the second rider from his saddle, while the others turned their horses around for cover.

Jake had already crossed the bottom and was halfway up the other side toward the trees. Lassiter turned to see Lonnie Hays and the rest of the gang coming over the top behind him.

Lassiter jumped on his stallion and started down the slope. Hays and the rest of the gang were starting down after him, with Hays yelling across at the other outlaws to turn around and start pursuing again.

Lassiter crossed the bottom and started up the other side as Jake began firing from the trees. Having left themselves in the open, the outlaws on the chalky hillside lost two more men to Jake's rifle. Lonnie Hays urged them forward, but they mounted hurriedly and retreated over the ridge.

The patch of pines was a welcome site as Lassiter urged his stallion up the remainder of the slope and finally into cover. He tied his stallion and hurried to where Jake and Lorna were crouched. Jake was pointing to the opposite side of the coulee, advising Lassiter that Hays and the other half of the gang had turned around toward the top once again.

"They don't want to get themselves shot up any more," Jake said with a smile. "Your idea worked."

"I'm just glad you can use a rifle like you can," Lassiter told Jake. "You don't do bad for riding a freight wagon and spitting tobacco juice most of the time."

Jake laughed and pulled at his suspenders. "I figured if I wanted to haul any more loads into this country, I'd best shoot pretty straight."

"There'll likely be some more to be done," Lassiter commented, watching Hays and the gang on the opposite slope.

The ridge across from him was lined with outlaws. Hays was sitting upon his horse impatiently with his men, while one of them pointed across the bottom. More had joined them since gathering the scattered horses, and those who had survived Lassiter's rifle along the chalk slope were back with the main group.

"They're thinking about going around us and attacking from different sides, aren't they?" Jake said, shielding his eyes from the sun.

"It appears that way," Lassiter agreed, watching Hays's arm pointing in various directions.

"We'll be trapped after all," Lorna said.

"No, we won't," Lassiter assured her. "They've got to travel a lot of country to get around behind us, too much to do it very quickly. They know that, and they're figuring all the angles. We'll just wait and see what they come up with."

Lassiter saw no need for immediate concern. Considering the position they were now in, the outlaws were at a distinct disadvantage. Coming at them head-on, the gang would be lined up for suicide. It was almost certain they wouldn't try that again.

But Lassiter realized that Lorna was right when she worried about them feeling too safe in the cover of the pines. The only water was what they had left in the canteens, and there was no other source nearby. They would have no choice but to leave as soon as it became apparent how the thieves were going to come at them.

Finally, two separate groups of outlaws split off from Hays and four other men. They rode in opposite directions in an effort to come around and close in on the trees along the ridge. As soon as they had gotten out of sight, Lassiter led the way to the horses.

"Now we make a run for it again," he said. "I don't think Hays and the men with him will start across at us until they see the rest of the gang closing in on our position. We're going to have to fight our way through one of the two bunches trying to surround us, but that's better odds than what we're facing right now."

Lorna and Jake both agreed, though they knew it was going to be dangerous. They wouldn't be able to just ride out of hiding without someone seeing them. Hays and the men with him wouldn't see them, but one of the other groups working their way around were bound to spot them sooner or later.

Lassiter again pulled Lorna up behind him, and they rode down from the pines, through a deep coulee and into a twisting bottom. Lassiter had spotted a series of gullies and ridges not far away that would afford them cover while they escaped the outlaws.

As they reached the first ridge, Lassiter spotted three

outlaws coming at them from a hill just across the twisting bottom. Two more were dismounting with their rifles.

Lassiter jumped down from his horse and told Lorna to get into the saddle and take the reins.

"What are you going to do?" Lorna asked.

"The same thing I did before," Lassiter replied. "But this time I'm going to get an extra horse for us."

Though Jake protested again, he finally turned his horse. Lorna urged Lassiter's stallion ahead, and the two rode through a steep draw toward a ridge on the opposite side. When they were halfway up the slope, Lassiter saw Lorna slip sideways from his stallion and fall backward down the slope.

Jake turned his horse around and rode down to assist Lorna. She appeared to be dazed, and Lassiter worried that perhaps she had hurt her head once again.

But there was no time for him to help her yet. Lassiter now turned his attention to the five outlaws. He worried more about the two on the ridge than the three riding toward him, and he set his sights on one just taking aim at him.

The rifles went off simultaneously. Lassiter heard the whine of a bullet as it narrowly missed his left shoulder. Lassiter's shot hit the outlaw, and he doubled over at the middle, tumbling down the clay slope and onto a rock outcropping.

The second outlaw was running for cover when Lassiter's bullet clipped him high in one leg. He went down and crawled over the ridge to cover on the other side.

Jake now had Lorna sitting up. He opened fire on the three outlaws riding at Lassiter. One of them pulled up, his left arm hanging useless. The other two kept coming, and Lassiter dropped one from the saddle as he came up and over a ridge just above his position.

The last outlaw turned his horse in retreat. He rode out of sight into a ravine and remained behind it for cover. Lassiter eased his way over to where the horse of one of the fallen outlaws was grazing and took the reins. Once in the saddle, he was soon with Jake and Lorna again.

"Are you hurt, Lorna?" he asked her. He then looked at Jake.

"I'm fine, just fine," Lorna said, staggering to her feet.

"Take it easy," Lassiter warned her.

"Don't worry about me, please," Lorna insisted. "That's a nice paint mare you've got there."

"She's yours to ride if you care to," Lassiter offered. "I'm sorry about my stallion."

"It wasn't his fault," Lorna said. "I was just looking behind and lost my balance, that's all. I'll be fine. Let's get going, so the rest of them don't catch us."

Lassiter thought that they probably had a good enough head start now to beat Lonnie Hays and the rest of the gang out of the badlands.

"We're going to make it now," Lorna said. "I know that." She climbed on the paint mare while Lassiter mounted his red stallion. Careful to stay below the ridge lines as much as possible, Lassiter led them through the maze of badlands until they were within sight of the Missouri.

"We've lost them," he said with a grin. "They might try to trail us, but they'll never catch us now."

Jake laughed, and Lorna sighed with relief. "I just want to find Lanna now," she said, "and get out of this country."

Lassiter nodded. "Let's go do it."

Lonnie Hays watched from a ridge while Waller loaded Gruber's body onto the back of a horse. More men killed by this stranger. Carson would have to be the one to contend with this man.

"I ain't about to let that stranger kill Gruber like that and just ride off," Waller said. "We can still catch them."

"You go catch him then," Lonnie said. "We've lost enough men as it is. Carson will have our hides for this. He can get that stranger."

"That stranger will be clean out of the country by the time Carson gets back," Waller protested. "I say we all go after him."

"I just told you we ain't going to do that," Lonnie reminded him. "How much plainer do I have to make it? Now, gather up the rest of the men, and let's get that roan stallion back to the hideout. At least we've got something to show Carson when he gets back."

Waller looked out into the badlands. His face was still clouded with anger. "Maybe I'll just go on after that stranger by myself," he said gruffly. "Nobody around here seems to care about Gruber or Jeff or any of the others. Nobody but me."

Lonnie Hays had turned his horse, but now he reined the animal back around. He glared at Waller.

"You take off after him, if you've got your mind made up. But you listen to me, and listen good: I don't care if you get that stranger or not. Don't show up back with this outfit though. Do you understand? You take off now, and you're on your own. You come back, and I'll kill you myself."

Lonnie turned his horse around again and started up the ridge. Waller stared at Hays's back for a time and turned again to look down into the badlands. Finally, he grunted and kicked his horse into a gallop up the ridge to join Hays and the rest of the gang. Waller knew that before it was all over, Lonnie Hays would wish he had taken everybody and stopped that stranger.

* * *

Charlie, the old ferry operator, smiled when he saw Lassiter and Lorna riding in with Jake Broden. He had wondered how long it would be until that stranger showed up again.

"Looks like you found one of those women," Jake called out to Lassiter, watching him dismount and help Lorna down from the paint mare. "I can't tell which one, though."

"This is Lorna," Lassiter said by way of introduction. "You can tell by her city clothes."

"That's all, I'd say," Charlie laughed. "You see another one that looks just like her, and you'll have your chores done."

"We had some chores to do before we could even get back down here," Jake interjected. "We met just about all the Hays Gang but one."

Old Charlie nodded. "Carson Hays. He was through here not long back. Headed for Fort Benton. He and some others of his gang. I didn't breathe too good while they were here." He pointed over to where a crude wooden cross was constructed over a mound just back from the river.

"I see you buried him after all," Lassiter commented.

"Not before I caught a mess of catfish with part of him. Couldn't use all of him, though. He got too ripe, and I had to bury what was left."

Lassiter noticed Lorna staring at him. "I'll explain it to you later," he promised her.

"If Carson Hays had even suspected who's in that grave," Charlie said, "you wouldn't be talking to me right now."

"It seems to me that just about everyone in the whole territory around here has nightmares about Carson Hays," Lassiter observed.

"You're the only man I've ever met who could know he was around and still sleep good," Charlie told Lassiter.

"I wish Carson Hays knew about you," Jake then said to Lassiter. "I wonder how he'd sleep."

Jake then went on to tell Charlie the story of their escape from Lonnie Hays and the majority part of the gang. He told Charlie that it was likely Will Carlson and the stranglers who were riding with him had gotten themselves killed by the thieves somewhere in the badlands.

"Have you seen any of them passing through here?" Jake asked Charlie.

Charlie lit his pipe. "No, but I heard they ain't been around Rocky Point, either. It could be you're right." He shook his head. "Hard country, this is."

"It's time I got Lorna out of here," Lassiter said.

"You been to Arrow Creek yet?" the old man asked.

"We're headed there right now," Lassiter told him. He looked at Jake and Charlie both, and shook their hands. "I certainly appreciate the help you two have been to me."

Lorna reached up and kissed Jake on the cheek. "Thank you so much for all your kindness," she told him. "I won't forget you."

Jake blinked and touched his cheek gently where Lorna had kissed him. "Thank you, ma'am," he said. "I won't forget you, either. You're the prettiest thing that ever set on my wagon seat." He touched his cheek again.

"That'll give you something to think about while you're driving that freight wagon of yours back to Fort Benton," Charlie told Jake. He reached over and touched the side of Jake's face. "That don't feel too bad."

"Don't be rubbing it off," Jake protested.

Lassiter helped Lorna back on the paint mare, then climbed on his stallion. After Charlie and Jake had wished them good luck, they took a trail out of the bottom.

They stopped at the crest of a hill to look back. Jake was leading his mules out of the corral to his freight wagon, while Charlie walked alongside, telling stories about his adventures in the ferry business.

"That's quite a pair, those two," Lassiter said. "It's a pleasure to know their kind."

"I wish all the men around here were like them," Lorna said.

Lassiter nodded. "Let's find your sister and get back to Fort Benton," he said. "We're apt to run into the worst kind of men out here."

Lorna nodded. "Carson Hays." She then looked at Lassiter. "You know, I've seen that man in my dreams. He was with Lanna, and he's the worst man there ever was."

"Let's get going," Lassiter said, "or we're bound to find out just how bad he really is."

13

CARSON HAYS LEANED OVER the bar and filled his glass once again. He tossed his head back and drained the shot glass, then poured another. He coldly eyed the bartender.

"I want you to tell me the way it happened," he said. "I want it all."

The bartender nodded nervously. "I'm telling you all I know. Ask anybody who was here that day. It happened right out front. I wasn't no part of it, though."

Hays grunted. His mind was trying to construct the events that had occurred out in front of the saloon some days back, when three of his men had fallen victim to some stranger no one had ever seen before. A stranger dressed in black had taken on his best men and, in less time than it takes to tell it, had them all under his control: two killed, one captured.

They didn't have a chance, is how the bartender was telling it. Hays couldn't believe it; three of his best men against a lone stranger and they didn't have a chance?

And he was thinking about his gray mule, which he had

found at the livery, without the supplies. That explained what had happened to the fourth man. According to the bartender, someone from town had stopped a horse with a body draped over it. The chances were better than even that this stranger had had a part in that, also.

The bartender moved back a step when Hays rose to his full height and continued to glare at him.

"Tell me again what this stranger looked like," Hays demanded.

"Tall. Wore two guns. Black handles. I told you all this before."

"You'll tell me as many times as I want. Understand?"

The bartender swallowed and nodded nervously. He was fully aware of the man he was speaking to. Carson Hays had a reputation all over the territory, but no lawman had ever caught him in any criminal act. That's why he was still thieving and killing: there were no lawmen around who wanted to catch him in the act. And anyone who had watched him steal horses or kill would never testify against him or his men.

"Where did this stranger come from?" Hays asked.

"Just drifted in," the bartender replied. "He and another stranger shot it out with them, right out front." The bartender pointed. "But don't ask me where those two are now. I know one of them took a couple of slugs, but I ain't seen either of them since that day."

"Which one got hit?" Hays asked.

"Not the stranger in black," the bartender answered. "It was the other one. That stranger in black was shooting faster than you could see."

Hays smiled glumly. A stranger who is good with a gun shows up, and suddenly everybody gathers courage. Hays poured another drink.

"You say he shot two of my men? What happened to the third one?"

"The stranger winged him," the bartender replied. "Then they took him to jail. But he tried to break loose and somebody shot him. They're up on the hill, all buried in the same grave. It weren't none of my doing."

"Who shot him when he tried to break loose?"

"I don't know. I never saw it, I swear."

Carson Hays slammed the shot glass against the bar. There wasn't much use in visiting the gravesite of men who would no longer do him any good. He figured his best move would be to take the gang members who had come with him and start back toward the hideout with the supplies.

This was going to cause a problem with searching for Lanna, and that angered Hays considerably. He would take it out on the stranger, when he found him.

Hays poured one last drink while the bartender watched. "You know where those two strangers are?" he asked the bartender.

"I can't say for certain," the bartender told Hays, "but I heard somebody say he thought the stranger was headed for Rocky Point."

"Why would he go there?"

"There's talk he's looking for a woman who looks like your wife."

"What?" Hays suddenly became very attentive. He leaned over the bar again. "What did you hear? And it had better be right."

"I don't know, other than what I heard. They say one of them had a picture of a woman who looked just like Lanna. They say she's a twin or something. I don't know nothing more, I swear."

Hays looked questioningly at the bartender. "A twin?"

"That's what they say. I don't know."

"What about the other stranger?"

The bartender shook his head. "Can't say. Maybe he went with the one in black."

"You're sure it was Rocky Point."

"That's what I heard. I'm only telling you what I heard."

Hays glared at the bartender and shoved the cork back into the bottle. "This was on the house. Right?"

"Sure, it was on the house." The bartender nodded nervously and backed away another step. "Hope you liked it."

Hays picked up the bottle. "I'll decide when I'm finished."

Hays turned from the bar with the bottle and rousted his men from their drinking at a nearby table. Once outside, he announced they were going back to the hideout via Rocky Point.

"We've got some business with a stranger dressed in black," Hays told his men. "Word is around that he's headed for Rocky Point, looking for a woman who looks just like Lanna."

The men looked at one another and back at Carson Hays. "Looks just like Lanna?" one of them said.

Hays nodded. "I don't know what to think. Lanna's supposed to have a twin sister who's up here. I intend to find out."

"What are we going to do about the two that shot up our men?" one of them asked. "I'd like to find them."

Hays stood thinking, fingering the shell casings sewn onto his vest. "The bartender said that stranger is the one who did the shooting," he finally said. "I'm going to find him. And if he's got Lanna with him, I'll make him die real slow."

*   *   *

Lassiter and Lorna rode toward Arrow Creek through a merciless midsummer sun. The open badlands were an oven, and water in the small draws was scarce. Lassiter had wisely filled the two canteens he always carried; but he and Lorna drank sparingly throughout the day, not knowing how far they might have to ride before they found good, fresh water.

Riding the steep terrain was difficult and trying for the horses. The clay banks were nearly straight up and down, and patches of grass and more level ground were hard to find. Deer trails were numerous, and Lassiter followed them as best he could.

Despite the treacherous country, Lassiter's stallion made good time, and the little paint mare Lorna now rode seemed bred for the task. Each draw and coulee seemed to open up into even more badlands, but they continued to ride through the parching heat with the knowlege they would soon see Arrow Creek.

Midafternoon brought them to an overlook that showed a twisting stream of water below. It was Arrow Creek. Lassiter looked at the map and judged them to be eight or nine miles from its mouth, deep in country that was seldom seen.

"If your sister is in here," Lassiter told Lorna, "she's certainly picked an excellent place to hide out. You would have to ride right up on someone in this kind of country to find them."

"It's steep getting down in there," Lorna observed. "Worse than where we were fighting the outlaws."

"We're here now," Lassiter told her. "We can take our time going down in. Nobody's chasing us."

"I hope not," Lorna said. "I'm tired of that."

Lassiter decided to take one last look around the country. The air was still and stifling hot. He squinted against the afternoon sun, through heat currents that rippled across the coulees and canyons. Visibility at a very long distance was blurred, but there seemed to be nothing else in the entire world but a sea of endless badlands.

"I can't think that anyone would have followed us now," Lassiter said. "Let's start down and see if we can find that cabin."

Lorna stared down at the looping flow of water below, and her face turned blank.

"What is it?" Lassiter asked her. "What's the matter?"

Lorna looked at Lassiter as if she didn't know him. Her eyes were blank once again, and Lassiter could tell that she was going through a bout with amnesia again. The fall from his stallion had hurt her.

He pulled the picture of Lorna and her husband from his pocket.

"You know who you are," Lassiter instructed her. "Your name is Lorna Jackson. Your husband, this man, is Darren Jackson. Do you remember?"

Lorna finally nodded. "What am I doing here, though?" she asked Lassiter.

"You want to find your twin sister," he told her. "Lanna is your twin sister. Remember her?"

"I don't know what I remember," Lorna said.

Lassiter handed her a canteen, and Lorna drank a few swallows.

"Everything is going to be just fine," Lassiter said, closing the canteen. "We're going to find your sister, and then we're going to go home. How does that sound?"

Lorna held her face in her hands. "My God, I don't know what to do. I don't understand this."

"You'll be back in Kansas City before you know it," Lassiter assured her. "Just hold on until we locate Lanna."

Lorna turned her head and looked behind them. "But she's in Rocky Point. I know she's in Rocky Point."

Lassiter had no idea how to make Lorna forget about Rocky Point. He'd had no prior experience with amnesia and could not understand why Lorna had gotten it into her head somehow that Lanna was in the little cowtown back along the Missouri. He realized it was doubtful that even Lorna, when and if she ever fully recovered, would know what had made her so sure about Lanna's whereabouts. But for now, he had to do his best to control her actions.

"We've got to get to Rocky Point," Lorna said again.

"No, your sister is not in Rocky Point," Lassiter corrected her. "She's supposed to be hiding out in a cabin somewhere along this small creek." He pulled the map from his saddlebag once again. "See? Do you remember seeing this before? Sure you do. I told you about the old man who knows this area so well."

Lorna blinked. "The cabin where she's hiding from the outlaws? From the one named Carson Hays."

Lassiter smiled. "That's right. You remember."

Lorna turned around on her horse again. "She's not at Rocky Point?"

"Lorna, you're going to have to forget about Rocky Point. We left there for good. Your sister is somewhere in these badlands, likely along this creek. You've got to believe me."

Lorna rubbed her forehead. "It's not that I don't believe you. It's just that I can't seem to focus on where I am at times, or even who I am."

"I don't know how to help you," Lassiter said. "I'll do the best I can, but you've got to trust me."

"You don't understand, Mr. Lassiter," Lorna told him, her expression pained. "When my memory fogs up, I don't know how to respond to anybody."

Lassiter nodded. "We'll just see if we can't locate your sister and get you both out of this country as soon as we can."

Lorna nodded and leaned over her horse toward Lassiter to look at the map. "Where do you think she is?"

Lassiter pointed up the creek a short ways. "According to the map, she's likely in a cabin that sits back around that little bend."

"I sure hope she's back there," Lorna said.

"We'll just ride down real slow," Lassiter told her. "That way, if she sees us right away, she won't think we're up to something. By the time she gets a good look at you up close, she'll have to wonder."

Lassiter led the way down a trail that angled its way to the bottom. The horses drank deeply in the creek, now reduced to a small current connecting large holes fed by underground springs. The water was cool, and they disturbed a pair of mourning doves resting in the shade of a cottonwood bough. The birds darted off, their singing wings beating a zigzag course along the creek bottom.

Lassiter watched the flight of the birds. He noted that as soon as they got near a little bend at the base of a hill, they veered off from their course of flight and up a draw into a tanble of buffalo berry.

"I don't know if it's your sister or not," Lassiter said to Lorna, "but somebody knows we're here. And they're waiting just around that bend." He pointed. "We've got to be careful."

"Then what are we waiting for?" Lorna asked eagerly.

"We don't want to get ambushed," Lassiter told her. "And if it's your sister, we don't want to alarm her. We'll ride along the trail that crosses over that little humpback across the creek."

Lassiter rode up onto the trail, with Lorna close behind.

He watched carefully, noting that there was a small cabin situated on a little beach across the creek. When they were directly across from the cabin, Lassiter stopped his stallion and held his hand up in a peace gesture.

"Lanna Hays?" he called out. "I've brought your twin sister to see you. We would like to talk to you."

There was no answer, and Lorna began to get worried.

"Why isn't she answering? Isn't she even there?"

"Just hang tight," Lassiter advised. "Anyone hiding out isn't going to jump out and greet the first two strangers that come along."

Lassiter continued to hold his hand up, calling out again. He was aware of the cover all around the perimeter of the cabin, where anyone could hide and not be detected. He also noted a heavy growth of willows along the creek where the mourning doves had veered off their flight pattern.

"Let's ride ahead just a little," Lassiter told Lorna. "Then we'll cross the creek and move toward the cabin."

With one hand still raised in the air, Lassiter rode a short ways ahead, then turned his stallion and crossed the creek. They came out on the far bank under a small rise. Whoever was in the willows could no longer see them.

"We'll wait here and see what happens," Lassiter told Lorna.

"What are we waiting here for?" Lorna asked. "Why don't we ride up to the cabin?"

"Just hold tight," Lassiter instructed her. "I'm trying to draw out whoever is in those willows. Let's get down and take cover."

Lassiter had no sooner gotten the words out than they

heard someone moving in the brush along the bank. Lassiter pulled one of his twin Colts.

"Don't," Lorna said.

"There's a gun barrel pointed at us," Lassiter said. "I saw a flash of sunlight against the barrel. We had better either take cover or find ourselves getting shot down right here and now."

14

LASSITER AND LORNA both froze as they heard a voice addressing them from the brush along the creek at their back.

"Don't move, either of you." It was a woman's voice. "I want you both to put your hands up in the air."

Lorna's eyes lit up. She started to turn around in the saddle.

"I said, don't move!" the woman yelled again. "I'll shoot the both of you before you can blink."

Lassiter raised his hands, but Lorna couldn't be contained. She turned in the saddle anyway.

"Lanna? Lanna, is that you?"

There was no response for a moment. Then the woman said, "How did you know my name?"

Lassiter turned slowly, watching the woman squinting at Lorna. They were still far enough away that the woman couldn't see Lorna too clearly. But it was obvious to Lassiter that the woman could see her well enough to notice their obvious resemblance to each other.

Lorna jumped down from her mare. "Lanna, I'm your sister, Lorna."

The woman, her long and flowing dark hair drawn back behind her ears, stepped out from the brush, holding a rifle.

"Stop where you are," she told Lorna. "I don't know what's going on here, but I won't hesitate to shoot you."

Lorna ignored her sister's threat and started to run toward her with arms outstretched. Lanna Hays held the rifle and stared. They were identical, despite Lanna's worn and dusty trail clothes. The closer Lorna got to her, the more her eyes widened.

"Who in the world are you?" the woman asked. "This is crazy. You look just like me."

"Lanna!" Lorna told her. "My God, it is you! It really is you!"

Lanna lowered the rifle and stood stunned. Lassiter dismounted and watched her as she dropped the rifle when Lorna jumped into her arms. Both women wiped tears from their eyes and looked one another over from head to foot.

Lorna talked as she studied her sister, detailing what she knew of their very early lives together and the incident on the Oregan Trail.

"I was told you had drowned," Lorna said. "That was so long ago."

"I don't remember a lot about my early childhood," Lanna said. "The folks who raised me said they found me near dead on the banks of the North Platte River. I do remember the water, but I must have gotten out somehow."

Lassiter listened while Lanna told how she had grown up an orphan, having no knowledge of her real family, but had always felt part of her was missing. All during her young life in the gold camps, she had wondered about herself and why she felt so all alone and distant from everyone else. Something in her life had always been missing.

"That's how I always felt," Lorna confessed. "Since we're identical twins, I guess we think alike in a lot of ways. I guess we are, in fact, part of one another. At least that's how I feel."

"I don't know how I feel," Lanna confessed. "Kind of funny, I guess. I still can't believe all this. How did you even know I was alive?" she asked. "And how in heaven's name did you ever find me way up here?"

"Have you ever heard of amnesia?" Lorna asked her.

"No," Lanna said, shaking her head.

Lorna then explained about her head injury and how she had acquired her problem with memory and with even knowing who she was a great deal of the time. Lanna listened with fascination as Lorna talked about the throw from her horse and later, the woman who had visited her husband's office.

"Didn't you ever get funny feelings, as though somebody who was a part of you was somewhere else?" Lorna asked her sister. "Didn't you ever have the feeling that you were someplace else, living some kind of life in your head that you couldn't quite see as being real, but knowing there was somebody like you living that life?"

Lanna nodded slowly. "You know, I have felt that way. But I felt I was somewhere I didn't want to be, trapped in some kind of place I wasn't used to. The feelings didn't make me feel good at all, so I forced them away whenever they would come. That happened a lot when I was growing up, but I haven't felt that way for some time now."

The two women then walked over to where Lassiter stood patiently.

"This is the man who helped me find you," Lorna told her sister. "His name is Lassiter."

Lassiter was aware of Lanna's confidence as she shook his hand and studied him thoroughly. Her eyes were bright, and she looked to be doing very well for someone who was running from a very dangerous man.

"It looks to me like you've made yourself quite at home here," Lassiter told her.

"I hold my own," she said. "You don't do too bad yourself. You know a little about tracking people, don't you?"

"A little," Lassiter said with a smile.

"How did you know I was here?"

"Old Charlie, down at Clagett's Landing, was a lot of help to me. Two outlaws had a map that I managed to finagle from them, and Charlie showed me the right cabin to look for."

Lanna looked at Lorna and back at Lassiter again. "You 'finagled' the map from some outlaws?"

Lassiter withheld his smile. "In a manner of speaking," he said. "I 'finagled' it from them after they proved to be not very neighborly."

"I understand," Lanna told him. "How many of the Hays Gang have you managed to *finagle* things from?"

"A lot of them," Lorna answered for him. "They're after him."

Lanna nodded. "I would imagine. It's funny you haven't run into Carson yet."

"I'm hoping to avoid that," Lassiter said. "I got into all this as a favor to a friend, and it's gotten out of hand."

"If Carson ever finds you, it will be you or him," Lanna warned Lassiter. "You know that, don't you?"

"I've known that since the first day I got into all this,"

Lassiter told her. "But this isn't the first time I've been in similar circumstances."

"I can well imagine," Lanna said, looking Lassiter over once again. "You hold your own, that's for sure. But you exposed your back to me, and I think you did it on purpose."

"You hadn't started shooting at us before that," Lassiter told her, "so I didn't think there was any reason to think you'd want to shoot us later."

"That's pretty trusting," Lanna said.

"When we came in here," Lassiter explained, "I didn't know what to expect from you. I realized before long, though, that you weren't all the outlaw and killer everybody talks you up to be. I just wanted to get you and Lorna together without making you worry about us for very long. By exposing our backs to you, that made it easy for you to get the drop on us."

Lanna smiled. "What I want to learn from you is how you knew I was hiding in that mess of willows on the other side of the hill."

"The doves," Lassiter answered. "Those two mourning doves that we jumped started to land near you and then took off up a draw."

Lanna nodded and smiled again. "It's good to have you on my side, Mr. Lassiter. How about if you and Lorna come up to the cabin? I can fix you some venison and coffee. I don't drink anything stronger any more."

Lorna looked at Lassiter and then at Lanna. "How long will it take you to pack?"

"Pack?"

"Don't you think we'd ought to be going?" Lorna asked her sister.

"Going?"

"We can catch up on our lost years once we're out of

here," Lorna continued. "We'd better get started to Fort Benton."

"There's no need to rush off," Lanna said. "I haven't even gotten to know you. You can stay for a little while."

"I don't think you understand," Lorna said. "There's no need to stay here and talk. We can talk anywhere. Get your things together. We've got the rest of our lives to talk."

Lanna looked confused. "What do you mean?"

"I want you to come back to Kansas City with me," Lorna replied.

"Kansas City? Where in God's name is that?"

"A long ways south of here," Lorna replied. "And we'd best get going out of here as soon as we can."

"I don't plan to go anywhere," Lanna announced.

"You mean you don't plan to leave here?" Lorna asked, unbelieving. "You don't intend to go back down to Kansas City with me?"

"What's in Kansas City that I don't have here?" Lanna asked. "There's no reason I would want to go down there."

Lorna was shocked. When she was finally able to speak, she repeated herself, as if she hadn't heard Lanna all along.

"You are coming back to my home to live with me, aren't you? Certainly you are." She reached for Lanna's arm.

It was Lanna's turn to blink. She stepped back from her sister. "I don't really know why I'd want to leave here," she said. "There's no place else I want to be."

"How can you want to stay up here?" Lorna pleaded. "That killer, Carson Hays, will find you sooner or later."

"I'm just waiting for him to find me," Lanna said. "There are already three of his men buried down by the creek. They found me. No one can come in here from any direction without me seeing them.''

"You are serious, aren't you?" Lorna said, shaking her head. "This is where you want to live? I can't begin to understand this, not at all.''

Lanna stretched her arm toward the hill around them. "This is my home, Lorna. Can't you see that? You wouldn't want to move up from Kansas City and live here, would you?''

"No. It would be impossible even if I did. My husband's law practice is in Kansas City.''

"I don't know what I would do in Kansas City," Lanna said. "I don't know anything about places like that. I doubt if I could learn to live in a place like that even if I wanted to.''

Lorna looked for a place to sit down and finally found a log near the creek. Lassiter and Lanna followed, and Lanna sat down next to her.

"I wish you would understand," Lanna said. "A big city is no place for me. I've never been to places like that, and I don't belong there. Don't you see that?''

Lorna was crushed, totally defeated. She sat silently on the log, staring out across the creek.

"Please, Lorna," Lanna begged, "don't be mad at me.''

"I wanted to find you because I knew you hadn't died, and I thought all along that I had to have you living with me to be a whole person," Lorna said. "I guess I won't ever be a whole person.''

"Nonsense. I'm a whole person, and you're a whole person," Lanna told her. "I'm certainly glad you found me and that we got to talk, but I'm my own person. You've got to make yourself a whole person on your own, like I did.''

Lorna looked at her sister. "Well, I guess I'll be doing that without your help." She stood up and looked at Lassiter. "I guess we'd better be on our way, then. It's a long ways back home." She stepped past Lanna in anger and strode to her horse with long, decisive steps.

Lanna didn't run after her. She knew there was nothing she could do to soothe her sister's feelings. Instead, she shook Lassiter's hand once again.

"Thank you, Mr. Lassiter, for bringing Lorna to see me. I didn't want to hurt her."

Lassiter could see moisture forming in Lanna's eyes as she blinked and turned again to watch Lorna climbing on the paint mare.

"Don't blame yourself," Lassiter told her. "There was no way to avoid it."

"Did you know I wouldn't want to go back with her?"

"I didn't give it much thought. I guess I should have. Maybe I could have said something to her so that she might have expected it. But she's never been out here around this kind of people, and her head injury doesn't make things any easier for her. She'll be fine, though."

"Well, I hope she gets back where she belongs in good shape," Lanna said, watching Lorna ride across the creek.

"I'd better catch her," Lassiter said. "Take care of yourself."

Lassiter hurried to his stallion and rode after Lorna. The little paint mare was climbing the trail out of the bottom and Lassiter remained silent until they reached the top.

"I'm sorry it turned out this way," Lassiter said, riding up beside her, "but Lanna knows nothing about big cities, and doesn't care to learn."

"I know, I know," Lorna said with irritation. "I don't need to hear it from you again." Then she took a deep breath. "I'm sorry, Mr. Lassiter. It's just that I can't believe I'm going to leave her out here. I came all this way for nothing."

"It's her choice," Lassiter told her. "That's the way it has to be."

"That doesn't make it any easier."

"You wouldn't want her to go with you all the way back to Kansas City and then have her decide she didn't like it. That would be worse."

"I don't know," Lorna continued to argue. "Nothing could be much worse than this."

"There's lots of things that could be worse," Lassiter told her. "For one thing, you might not have ever found Lanna. Then you would never have known whether she was alive or dead."

"I suppose you're right," Lorna agreed. "I should be happy that she's alive and well, and that she's living her life the way she wants to."

"That's the way you have to look at it," Lassiter told her. "Every woman is entitled to decide what's best for herself."

"I guess what's best for me is to get back to my husband as quickly as possible," Lorna said.

15

BEN MORRIS SAT UP in bed and loosened the bandages on his leg. The bullet wound was healing nicely, and he was getting tired of being bedridden. Lying on his back had brought him too many concerns about what was happening with Lassiter and his search for Lorna Jackson.

The doctor had told him the day before he would need another week before he could ride, but Morris was now thinking of ignoring the advice and heading out for Rocky Point. He hadn't seen Lassiter since just after their gunfight with the outlaws in front of the saloon, and he wasn't sleeping well.

He had no idea how Lassiter was doing in his search for Lorna, but felt instinctively that something had gone wrong. Lassiter should have returned with Lorna before now.

Morris was also worried about Lorna's husband, Darren Jackson. He had promised to send telegrams to Jackson periodically about how the search for Lorna was going. Since getting himself shot up, Morris hadn't been able to keep his promise, and he knew Jackson would be concerned.

As Morris inspected his leg wound once again, he made up his mind to head into the badlands. He could ride, he was confident of that, and he didn't think the wounds would give him that much trouble. There had been no bleeding or seepage of any kind for over four days, and he felt healthy. His arm was doing equally well and, although both wounds would need a little longer to heal completely, Morris didn't figure he had the luxury of time.

As Morris considered leaving, someone knocked loudly at the door. The volume startled him. The doctor always announced himself before entering, but never with such force.

After climbing back under the blankets, Morris called to the visitor to come in. His eyebrows raised when Darren Jackson stepped through the door.

"No wonder I haven't heard from you," Jackson said. "I thought something had happened, so I broke away and traveled up here."

Morris, still startled, asked, "How in hell did you find me, Darren?"

"I rode to Helena first and found out you hadn't tried to send any new telegrams since the last one. From that telegram, I knew you'd come up here, so I took a chance. The story of your shootout with the outlaws is still being told around town."

Morris climbed out of bed and told Jackson the entire story while he dressed, including Lassiter's involvement. Jackson seemed somewhat relieved that a man of Lassiter's caliber was looking for Lorna, even if it was someone he didn't know. If Morris recommended this Lassiter fellow that highly, there was no reason to think he couldn't do the job. But he was worried about some other news he had heard.

"There is also talk that a bandit gunfighter was in one

of the saloons and is pursuing your friend,'' Jackson told Morris. "I'm worried that Lorna might get in the middle of something dangerous.''

"Was this gunfighter's name Carson Hays?'' Morris asked.

"That's the name,'' Jackson said with a nod. "What does all this mean?''

"It means,'' Morris said, reaching for his gun, "that Lorna has found the meanest bunch of thieves in this part of the country. Her sister was once married to that outlaw, so there's big trouble ahead.''

"Thieves? Lorna? I don't understand.''

"I'll explain it to you on the trail,'' Morris said, starting for the door. "I want to be out of here and at the livery stable before the doctor finds out I've left. He doesn't want me up and around yet, but there's no choice. We've got to get to Rocky Point as soon as possible.''

With Fort Benton still a full day's ride through the badlands, Lassiter and Lorna gathered wood in the twilight. Lassiter was soaking dried venison and beans in water. A small frying pan he always carried would provide them with their first hot meal since the chicken at the Fourth of July celebration in Rocky Point.

Lorna was starting to act strangely again. He was beginning to see clearly that Lorna and Lanna, being identical twins, were somehow attached emotionally, though Lanna had obviously learned to live more as an individual than Lorna. The way it looked now, Lorna was going to have a very difficult time accepting the fact that her sister wanted nothing to do with the big city.

Lassiter knew that Lorna would never live in the badlands. The two women, though alike in many respects, were adapted to totally different environments.

Before stopping to make camp, Lorna had commented that she wished they would hurry so that she could see her sister. At the time, Lassiter had been able to convince her they had already found Lanna and that they had talked to her extensively.

But there was no way of knowing what was going on in Lorna's mind, and Lassiter kept his eye on her while he began cooking.

"I'm sorry you're still disappointed in your sister," he told her, "but it seems to me that you've got a good life ahead of you."

Lorna stared at him. "Why would I be disappointed in my sister?"

"She wants no part of Kansas City. Remember?"

Lorna frowned, then nodded. She let out a deep breath. The memory of her meeting with Lanna had reappeared in her mind.

"You remember her saying that she wanted to stay in the badlands?" Lassiter asked her.

"Yes, I remember that now," Lorna said with a nod. "I was so disappointed."

"You shouldn't dwell on it, though," Lassiter advised. "Look ahead to your own life. You have a lot to live for."

"I suppose that's true," Lorna said, staring into the fire. "It's just that I had wanted Lanna to come back with me so badly. I still feel a part of me is missing without her."

"You have to learn to think like your sister," Lassiter told her. "You have to realize that you don't need anyone but yourself to make your happiness."

"I suppose that's true in a way," Lorna conceded. "At least, Lanna seems to prove that."

"She certainly proves it," Lassiter concurred. "Why do you think she's as content as she is?"

"I don't know," Lorna said. "I can't imagine. I can't believe she would be living all alone in a rundown cabin way out here and like it."

Lassiter stirred the venison and beans. "She has come to understand herself out here," Lassiter explained. "Whether she were living in a cabin or a castle, she would be working to make herself happy."

"But she's had a life much more difficult than I have," Lorna said. "How could she possibly be happy?"

"I don't know if you should think of it as just *happy*," Lassiter explained. "She's found a way to make herself peaceful inside."

"Peaceful?" Lorna said with a frown.

"Peace or contentedness," Lassiter replied with a nod. "When a person is alone and can enjoy life that way, without depending on other people and other things for happiness, then that person has truly found peace."

"Peace?" Lorna said quickly, as if the true meaning of the word had just struck her. "What do you mean by *peace?* I doubt if Lanna has experienced any peace during her entire life. Especially now. She's been fighting outlaws."

Lassiter looked up from the skillet. "I'm talking about peace within herself," he said. "She's found a life by herself out here, and she's at peace with that. She certainly has to take care of herself, and she has obviously had to kill at times to save her own life, but she still feels content."

Lorna stared at Lassiter. "You seem to understand my sister very well, don't you? How do you know so much about all this?"

"It's taken me some time to see that things can't be forced," Lassiter told her. "Once you decide you can make things as good as you want to by trusting they will be good, you can find peace. Sometimes it takes living in the wilderness to bring a person some peace."

Lorna shook her head. "I certainly don't understand you at all, Mr. Lassiter. I can't see how this kind of country could bring anybody anything like peace. It's full of outlaws and wild animals. The trails will kill you if you don't watch your step. I don't even know what it is that you're trying to tell me."

"I can't tell you," Lassiter said. "It's something you have to learn on your own."

"Do you think I'd live out in country like this to learn about what you're saying?"

"It's not likely."

"It's more than not likely," Lorna said, her voice heating up. "It would never happen."

"All I'm asking you to do," Lassiter explained, "is to let your sister lead her own life and to continue with your own. There's no reason to do anything else. Here, have a plate of beans and venison."

Lorna took the plate and forked through her food. "I'm not really hungry," she finally said, setting the plate down.

"You'll need the strength," Lassiter told her.

Lorna ignored Lassiter's suggestion to eat. "I'm so tired," she said. She got up and walked over to her bedroll. "I just want to rest for a while. That's all. Just rest."

Lassiter watched her lie down and place her head against a folded saddle blanket. The air was still very warm, and once in a while she would wipe a bead of sweat from her brow. Despite the heat, she readily fell asleep.

Lassiter ate his portion and left Lorna's in case she awakened later and decided she was hungry. He washed his plate and doused the fire with river water, occasionally looking over at Lorna, who was tossing and turning in her sleep. There was really nothing he could do for her, he concluded. She was going to have to work things out for herself.

Before retiring himself, Lassiter checked the hobbles on the horses. If he could just get Lorna back to Fort Benton, he thought, Ben Morris could take her from there back to her home. That's what she needed most, just to leave all of this behind her.

Carson Hays stopped with his men to water the horses. A nearly full moon was rising over the badlands, bringing the trails from total darkness into scattered light and shadow.

Hays thought only of Rocky Point and Lanna, and of the stranger he had heard about, a stranger who had handled himself against his best men. Who was this man? He wanted to find him.

There was no telling what other damage this stranger might do, especially if he was traveling with a woman who looked just like Lanna. It was still hard for him to consider that Lanna had a sister, an identical twin.

They had come a long way since leaving Fort Benton but Hays still wasn't ready to make camp for the night. He knew the men didn't like it, for various reasons, but no one had objected. He expected to hear soon from a man named Longham, however, who seemed to be getting impatient with the way things were being handled.

Hays cracked a little smile when they stopped at a crossing to water the horses and Longham finally spoke up.

"We've been doing a lot of nothing these past days," Longham commented. "I wished we could find some horses to take."

Hays looked at the outlaw, whose face was bathed on one side with white light. "I ain't worried about getting more horses just now. I've got a lot of things to settle before we start after horses again.''

"There ain't nothing we can do about your concerns," Longham continued. "We ain't helping much, I'd say.''

Hays glared at the man. "What are you beefing about?''

"It's just that lately all we've done is run around for what *you* want," Longham blurted. "We ain't gone after any horses or sold the ones we got in Canada. I just think that me and the rest of the boys ain't getting a fair shake, that's all. I mean, we ain't getting paid for running around with you. Ain't that right, boys?'' He looked around to the others.

Hays looked around to the rest of the outlaws as well. No one said a word. All had their eyes turned away from Hays, shooting glances through the semidarkness at Longham, as if to warn him that he was just asking for trouble.

"So, you don't think you're getting a fair shake, is that it?'' Hays asked Longham. "You'd rather not do what I tell you to do. Is that what you're saying?''

Longham began to fidget in his saddle. "I just meant that me and the boys could do more good if we just went off and got some horses, that's all. You can go do what you want. I just thought we should get back to work.''

"You know damn well that nobody goes off and gets horses unless I'm along," Hays told the outlaw. "Nobody! What the hell is wrong with you?''

"I didn't mean to rile you none," Longham said quickly. "I just thought—''

"You thought what? You thought you could buffalo me into letting you go after horses and then sell them yourself? Is that it?''

Longham's eyes widened. "No! I didn't mean that at all. No, I wouldn't do that.''

"The hell you wouldn't!" Hays yelled. Before Longham could speak again, Hays pulled his pistol and fired twice into the outlaw's midsection. Longham gasped and then yelled. His horse shied, and he tumbled off into the river.

The other men stared as Longham lay on his side, trying to keep his head above the level of the flowing water. No one dared dismount to help him. They could only watch as he fought to keep his head up.

Longham fought gamely, but finally succumbed to weakness. His head went under and he lay still, with only his shoulder and a part of his hip above water, and the moonlight shining off the water-slick clothes.

Hays holstered his pistol. "Anybody else wanting to sell horses behind my back?"

No one spoke. Hays stared down at Longham for a time and looked from man to man.

"Why don't somebody say something?" he went on. "Don't you all see that I've got to keep some kind of order here? It really don't have nothing to do with Lanna. I don't care about her one whit. Can't you all see that? She ain't got no right to just go off like that, though. She ain't going to get away with that!"

Hays realized he wasn't going to get anyone to comment. He grunted in disgust and finally told one of the men to grab the reins of Longham's horse.

"Let's get going," Hays said. "We've got to find Lanna and some stranger who thinks she belongs to him now. We've got to teach him different."

16

LASSITER OPENED HIS EYES and sat up. The moon was nearly full and silvery white overhead. Everything appeared calm and normal, though he didn't feel calm. He knew something nearby had awakened him.

Lassiter had been sleeping soundly, and he wondered if what had startled him had in any way been associated with a dream. He recalled being somewhere along a river where a flock of crows—omens of fate—had been passing overhead. They were circling him when some kind of noise resembling explosions under a blanket had startled the birds and sent them flying in all directions, bringing him awake at the same time.

He knew the dream had occurred within his sleep—the river flowing and the crows flying overhead had been inside his unconscious mind. He was just as certain the muffled explosions had been something separate from his sleep.

He stood up and looked around, the uneasiness within him growing steadily stronger. The night was filled with the frogs croaking in nearby puddles and coyotes calling from the hilltops. Nothing of this nature had awakened him, he knew, for he wasn't disturbed by natural sounds. It had been sounds that didn't normally belong there which had awakened him.

Lassiter paced for a time, trying to recall what he might have heard in his sleep. He thought hard, and it suddenly came to him. He realized he had heard gunshots.

Now he wondered from which direction they had come and from how far away. There was no way of telling. Gunshots so late at night certainly meant trouble.

Lassiter noted that the fire still smoldered. Smoke would be reaching out from camp; and with the absence of wind, likely in all directions. It was time to move.

"Lorna, wake up." Lassiter shook her from her fretful sleep.

"What is it?"

"Let's saddle the horses," he told her. "We have to move camp, right away."

"What's wrong?" she asked.

"I think I heard gunfire," he told her. "I don't want to alarm you, but we can't take any chances."

Lorna stood up and rubbed sleep from her eyes. Lassiter disappeared into the darkness and reappeared shortly, leading the horses.

"You can go back to sleep once we've moved," he told Lorna, taking the saddle blanket she had been using as a pillow. "We'll just mosey off this main trail, and then we can rest easy."

"That won't be easy now," she said, watching him throw the blanket over the back of her mare. "Not after you awakened me and told me to wait to go to Rocky Point."

Lassiter turned. "What?"

Lorna was now looking out into the night. "Rocky Point," she repeated. "It's not fair that you told me to wait again."

Lassiter finished saddling the mare and started on his stallion. There was silence, except for the frogs. The coyotes had stopped howling.

"I've got to get to Rocky Point," Lorna said, breaking the silence.

"Lorna, how many times do we have to go over that?" Lassiter said, with an edge to his voice.

Lassiter's stallion began neighing, as did the mare. He watched the two horses prick up their ears and look straight out into the darkness.

"Horses coming," Lassiter said. "They're close by, real close by. In fact, I can hear them."

"Who could it be?" Lorna asked.

"I don't know. I should have been paying closer attention."

"They're outlaws, aren't they?" Lorna said, peering into the shadows.

"It would seem that way," Lassiter agreed, "or they would be calling into camp by now to announce themselves."

"What are we going to do?" Lorna asked. She was clutching Lassiter's sleeve.

"I'm going to get you into hiding and ride out from camp," Lassiter told her. "That way I can get them out into the open, and at least we'll have a chance."

As the riders drew ever closer, Lassiter handed Lorna the reins to her horse and she followed him downriver a ways and into a thicket of willows and young cottonwoods that was almost too thick to walk in.

"You stay right here," Lassiter said, his voice urgent. "I'll be back when I get us free of them."

"How are you going to take care of yourself alone?" Lorna asked.

"I'll manage," Lassiter told her.

"Don't go," Lorna begged. "They'll find me."

"Not if you stay quiet," he said. He showed her how to hold the muzzle of her horse to avoid more neighing. "Just stay calm and keep hiding until I get back. I'll decoy them out of camp."

"Please! *Don't leave me!*"

"I have to," Lassiter hissed. "Don't you understand? There's no other way. We're trapped here otherwise. Just sit tight like I told you. I'll be back."

Panic-stricken, Lorna tightly gripped the mare's muzzle and held her breath.

She could hear Lassiter jumping on his stallion, followed by strong hoofbeats as the animal surged into a run. When he was out a ways from the river, she heard the sounds of gunfire and men yelling. She wanted to scream with fright, but controlled herself. She just knew Lassiter had been shot, and that they were very soon coming for her. She buried her face against the mare's neck and wept silently.

Lassiter was riding out from the edge of camp, his stallion almost in full stride. He opened fire on two men he had surprised in front of him, both of whom were trying to shoot him from their startled horses.

He saw one of them fall as he lowered himself over his stallion's back and plowed through a section of small willows between the two riders. The other outlaw was having trouble staying on his horse and lost the opportunity for another shot.

Lassiter breathed just a little easier. There were more, he knew, and he would have to face them, too.

Soon he was out in the open, riding as hard as he could through the darkness, with riders behind him. To his right another outlaw appeared, a bouncing shadow on a dark horse with a pistol gleaming in the moonlight. The outlaw began shooting at Lassiter, as he spurred his horse straight toward him.

Lassiter returned the fire three times. The outlaw was holding his chest and slumping as Lassiter's stallion collided with his horse, sending the creature into a twisting fall.

Without breaking stride, Lassiter's stallion continued across the open. The gunfire behind him ceased as the distance between him and the oncoming riders increased. Before long, his pursuers were nothing more than moving black dots amidst rolling shadow and moonlight.

Lassiter realized that he didn't want the outlaws giving up on him, not just yet. He wanted to lead them as far as he could from Lorna's hiding place. She would be nearly crazy with fear by now, and he didn't want them contemplating their losses where she could hear them.

Lassiter slowed his stallion down, and when the riders were close enough to see him, he jumped down and picked up a hoof, as if he were inspecting a shoe. Then he hurried back into the saddle and turned his horse up a draw.

The outlaws reached the mouth of the draw and began shooting at him again as he rode over the crest of a hill. They were coming with renewed vigor now, Lassiter realized, and would come until they finally learned he had tricked them.

Lassiter urged his stallion through a series of hills and gullies, making a large circle back around toward the river. He stayed close enough to keep the outlaws' interest, but far enough to keep himself out of jeopardy. After a time, he saw them no more and knew they had gotten wise to his trick.

Lassiter reined in his stallion and watched behind. In the distance, he could see riders going over a steep hill back toward the main trail. He could rest assured now they had finally given up the chase. It was time to get back to Lorna.

Carson Hays sat his horse in the moonlight and fumed. His men were all talking among themselves, some of them angry, some of them fearful. One of the outlaws lay draped over a horse. He would be of no more use to Hays. What could he do about losing all his men?

Two of those who hadn't been shot were off their horses, attending to one who had been badly wounded through the chest and was now lying beside the trail. His horse had been in a collision and was just off the trail, walking in dazed circles and limping.

Hays breathed through gritted teeth and contemplated his next move. He hadn't expected what had just occurred. In fact, he was having trouble believing it had all happened. He had led many a raid against a calm night camp for looting and killing, but nothing like this had ever happened before.

This rider had come at them like the devil himself. No one had expected that. And then, feigning a lame horse just to get them off the main trail and lost in the rugged stuff—what was that all about?

Hays only knew he had been made a fool of, and he didn't like it one bit. If he wasn't so pressed for time, he would make sure he and his men chased this rider down, whoever he was, and made him pay for what he had done.

But now there was the wounded outlaw to consider, and also his search for Lanna.

"You'd better look at Clements," one of the men said to Hays, turning from the fallen outlaw.

"What do I want to look at him for?" Hays asked.

"I ain't doing so good, Carson," the wounded outlaw choked. "I'd like to get back to Fort Benton to a doc, if you don't mind."

Hays looked from the back of his horse through the shadows along the trail. He fingered the shell casings attached to his vest and gritted his teeth again.

"You hear me, Carson?" Clements managed. "I need a doc bad."

Hays remained silent while his men looked to one another. They remembered well what had happened back at the crossing when they had been watering the horses. They had seen one of their number blatantly killed for expressing his opinion. None of them felt safe now.

It occurred to them that their leader was becoming more obsessed with locating Lanna and somehow exacting revenge than he was with his men and their welfare. No one had ever asked for any special privileges, but everyone had joined the gang with the notion of making money by stealing horses. They hadn't been doing a lot of that lately.

The wounded outlaw tried to rise up from the ground, but fell back again and choked on blood.

"You think you could stand the trip back to Fort Benton?" Hays finally asked the outlaw.

"I got no choice," Clements answered. "I got a bullet in my lungs and I got no other way to get it out."

Hays looked at one of the outlaws on the ground with him. "You take him back to Fort Benton, Benson," he ordered. He told the other man on the ground to help Benson get Clements onto his horse.

"You want me to go with him alone?" Benson asked.

"That's what I said," Hays told him sternly.

"What about that rider who shot us up?" Benson asked, fear evident in his voice.

"What about him?" Hays asked. "You ride straight for town and you won't meet him."

Everyone was silent. Hays knew full well that the rider was likely this mysterious gunfighter dressed in black that they had all heard so much about in Fort Benton. Benson, as well as the rest of his men, were scared to death of this man. They all wondered if he wasn't going to leap out of the shadows on his big horse once again, and shoot more of them down.

Hays didn't know what to make of all this. Never before had he seen his men react this way. They had come up against some Mounties up in Canada and had shot it out without losing a man. Occasionally a stock owner would put up a feeble fight to protect his property, but he always died for his stupidity. Somehow, things had changed.

Hays didn't allow himself to think of this gunfighter as any threat to him. He wished he had been close enough to get a shot off himself. He wondered what he would have felt had he been among those of his men who had come face to face with this man.

Hays watched the two men struggle to get the injured outlaw onto his horse. He coughed and moaned and made a mess of both men's clothes. When they finally got him tied into the saddle with a rope, Hays called Benson over to talk to him.

"I don't want you going very far," Hays told him. "Get back to the crossing and dump him. Then come back."

"What?"

"You heard me. Take him to where I shot Longham and leave him there in the water with him. We haven't got time for you to take him clear back to Fort Benton. We've got lots of work to do."

"You mean we're going to go after horses again?"

Hays's breath rattled. "When I say so! When are all of you going to get that through your heads?"

Benson didn't want to argue. He valued his life and knew Hays would take it in a snap if he didn't do just what he was told. He would take Clements and head for Fort Benton, he thought to himself, and maybe he wouldn't stop at the crossing where Longham had been shot. Maybe he would go on to Fort Benton anyway. Then he would just ride on, and he wouldn't ever come back.

17

LASSITER RODE DOWN a steep hill into a stream bottom choked with sagebrush and greasewood half as high as his stallion. Had he known about this place, he would have camped here instead of along the river. It would have afforded a great deal of cover and been safer than right down next to the main trail.

He thought about Lorna and wanted to reach her as quickly as possible. He rode down the bottom and came out along the main trail just above where they had made camp. As a matter of precaution, he decided to walk in.

Lassiter tied his stallion in the darkness and eased his way back into camp. The campfire was still smoldering, sending thin lines of smoke into the night.

He stood for a moment and listened intently. There was no wind whatsoever, and the air was still very warm from the day's heat. The only sound was the croaking of frogs in puddles up and down the creek.

He wanted to call out for Lorna, but held up. He heard horses coming along the trail just outside of camp.

It was one of the outlaws, leading a horse with another outlaw hunched over the saddle. The rider had no idea Lassiter was there and dismounted to check on the other man. He found the other man had died.

Lassiter watched while the outlaw untied the body and let it fall to the ground.

Lassiter stepped through the shadows and leveled one of his Colts. "Hold your hands up in the air."

The startled outlaw jumped and let out a yell.

"Just move easy," Lassiter warned, "unless you want to end up like your friend, there."

"Don't shoot me," the outlaw begged. "I don't aim to make no trouble for you."

"It's a little late for that, don't you think?" Lassiter asked him. "You and that whole bunch have made a lot of trouble for a lot of people already."

"I don't want no part of them anymore," the outlaw said. "Just don't shoot me."

"We're going to have a little talk," Lassiter said to him. "You just walk ahead of me out into the moonlight."

Lassiter herded the outlaw out of the trees and into the open, where the moonlight was reflected off a worried face.

"What are you going to do with me?" the outlaw asked.

"Just answer my questions," Lassiter said. "Are you part of the Hays Gang?"

"I told you I used to be," the outlaw said. "I told you I don't want no part of them anymore."

"Was Carson Hays leading you and the others tonight?"

"Yeah, Carson Hays was leading us," he replied nervously. "But he ain't sane no more. He's gone plumb crazy."

"Where's he at now? And the others?"

"They went on ahead. Carson made me start back to Fort Benton to get him to a doc." He pointed to the body on the ground. "I was supposed to meet them all in Rocky Point after I left him in town."

"Why were you all traveling at night?" Lassiter asked him. "What's the rush?"

"We all know about you. Carson wants you dead. We were on our way back to Rocky Point to find you."

"How did you know about me?" Lassiter asked him.

"We went to Fort Benton to get the four that were sent after supplies. We heard how you shot them up. The bartender told Carson everything."

Lassiter thought about Ben Morris and wondered if Hays and the others had managed to locate him.

"Did Hays and the rest of you look for the man that was with me?" Lassiter asked.

"No, we came straight out toward Rocky Point," the outlaw answered. "Like I said, Carson Hays has gone plumb crazy. He just up and shot one of us a ways back." He pointed back up the trail through the darkness. "He just shot him for something he said. All he cares about is finding that woman he used to own."

Lassiter nodded. "You say the bartender told Hays everything. Did he mention Lanna's twin sister?"

"Yeah. Is that true?"

"I'll show you," Lassiter said. With his pistol he motioned for the outlaw to move ahead of him slowly. A ways down the river, Lassiter stopped him. He was at the location where he had left Lorna, but there was no sign of her or her horse.

"Lorna? Are you in there? You can come out now. It's safe."

There was no response, and Lassiter moved closer to the tangle of trees and brush. If she was in there, he would certainly be able to see her by now. But there was no sign of any life or movement. She was gone.

"You hid her there?" the outlaw asked.

Lassiter didn't answer him, but looked around in the darkness, wondering why he had decided to leave her alone. He knew there had been no other way. He turned and saw the outlaw staring at him.

"Yes, Lanna really has a twin sister," he told the outlaw. "And, yes, I did hide her right here. You can think I'm crazy if you want, but she's gone."

Lassiter knew he didn't have to explain anything to this man, but he was beginning to ask himself how he had gotten involved in something like this. Lorna was so unpredictable; and just when he thought he had her safely on the way back to Ben Morris, something like this had to happen.

"Where'd she go?" the outlaw asked Lassiter.

"I don't know," Lassiter said, still holding his gun on the outlaw. "I'll have to go find her." He was thinking about where to begin.

"Well, it don't matter to me none," the outlaw said. "I told you, I'm finished with the Hays Gang. Just let me go."

Lassiter turned and looked at the outlaw, deciding what to do with the man. His priority was to find Lorna, and this outlaw would just slow him down. He didn't want to shoot him outright, and tying him up would do little good if there were more outlaws around to untie him.

"You're going to quit the gang?" Lassiter asked him.

"I'm through with them."

"Where will you go?"

"Out of this country, as quick as I can."

"Get out of here," Lassiter then said. "Start doing something you won't get killed over."

Without wasting another moment, the outlaw turned and ran to his horse. He didn't bother to even look behind him as he mounted and rode out at a full run. Lassiter noticed, as he started for his stallion, that the outlaw was not headed for Fort Benton. He was instead riding his horse at full speed along the trail toward Rocky Point.

Lorna rode the little mare as hard as she could without tiring the horse completely. The horse negotiated the hills and gullies with precision, jumping around and over clumps of sagebrush and saltbush that presented themselves as black humps in the moonlight.

Once she got to Clagett's Landing, she stopped for a time to rest the mare. She had been disoriented before, but was even more so now from the rugged miles of bouncing in the saddle. Though the landing looked familiar to her, she couldn't exactly place where she was.

Old Charlie seemed to suddenly form himself at her side. It scared her and she yelled.

"What in the name of creation are you doing here at this hour?" he asked her, pulling up a suspender. "Where's that stranger?"

Lorna backed away from him, letting the reins of her horse fall to the ground. She turned and ran for the trees.

"I don't aim to hurt you none!" Charlie yelled after her. "You know that."

Lorna ran into the cover of trees near the shore and found herself a thicket of willows. She slid into the tangle and sat with her hands over her face, remembering how she had hidden before, farther back along the river. She remembered the fear and the worry over the outlaws, and something popped inside her memory.

She pulled her hands away from her eyes and looked out into the night. It was as if she was a different person. She suddenly realized that it had been Lassiter who had placed her in hiding back along the river.

Now it came back to her. The fear had built up within her while she was in hiding. All the shouting and shooting had scared her and brought her out, like a young deer from cover, and she had ridden into the darkness, wanting only to get away from the terrible feeling that somebody was going to find her.

She peered through the brush, seeing Old Charlie on the bank, calling for her to come out. The little mare, having filled herself with water, stood grazing nearby in the moonlight.

Lorna remembered more, that she had been with Lassiter and that, as Charlie had mentioned, he was not with her now. She couldn't remember whether or not she had talked with him after he had placed her in hiding. She thought she hadn't. She realized she had just jumped on the little mare and had ridden as fast as she could away from there.

She wondered where Lassiter was now. No doubt he was looking for her. She suddenly felt very vulnerable without him. It also occurred to her that she must have ridden off without knowing where Lassiter or the outlaws were at the time. She began to cry.

Along the bank, Old Charlie called a couple more times for her to come back, that he had no intention of hurting her and was sorry for having scared her. Lorna dried her eyes and worked her way out of the willows.

"What in tarnation's happened?" Old Charlie asked her when she got back to the bank. "Did the Hays Gang kill that gunfighter?"

Lorna shook her head no.

"They didn't get him? Where is he?"

Lorna's head hurt, and she put her hands to both cheeks, digging into the flesh under the eyes with her fingernails.

Everything was tangled once again. Her mind was doing cartwheels.

"Are you feeling okay?" Charlie asked.

"I've got to get to Rocky Point," Lorna told him. "I've got to find Lanna."

"Lanna? You didn't find her? Where's that gunfighter?"

Lorna was throwing the reins over the neck of her mare. "I've got to find Lanna," she repeated. She swung into the saddle. "I've got to find Lanna."

Charlie reached for the reins. "Hold on a minute. Let me help you."

Lorna turned the horse before Charlie could clutch the reins. She hastily kicked the mare into a gallop, leaving Charlie calling her on the bank.

Benson dug his spurs into his exhausted horse. He could see the outline of Carson Hays and the rest of the men against the moonlit slope of a steep hill. They were all stopped, their necks craned, watching his approach.

Benson reined his horse in. "Carson, listen—"

"You about got yourself shot, you know that?" Hays broke in. "What the hell you riding like that for?"

"I've got news," Benson told Hays. "You ain't going to believe this."

"I thought you took Clements to Fort Benton," one of the other men interjected.

"Shut up!" Hays yelled at the outlaw. He turned back to Benson. "What news?"

"I stopped because Clements died," Benson began. "Then I was jumped by that gunfighter, the one who shot us up. He told me that Lanna *does* have a twin sister," Benson continued. "She was hiding all the time in the brush along the river. But he couldn't find her."

Hays was listening intently. "That gunfighter went back down to the river to get Lanna's sister from hiding?"

"Yeah, but he couldn't find her," Benson repeated. "I was there. He don't know where she went."

"Are you saying he was holding a gun on you and looking for this twin sister of Lanna's?" Hays asked.

"Yeah, but she wasn't where he left her. I say if we can find—"

"Why'd he let you go?" Hays broke in again. "Why didn't he shoot you, or hang you?"

Benson shrugged. "I don't know. I guess he didn't want to kill me."

"He didn't want to kill you? He sure as hell wanted to kill the rest of us."

Benson became confused. He had come back trying to get Hays to listen to a plan of his. But he hadn't been able to say a word yet.

Hays studied Benson some more. He spoke his thoughts out loud.

"You didn't make some kind of deal with that gunfighter, did you?" Hays asked. "If he let you go, you would set me up?"

"Hell, no!" Benson blared. "I wouldn't do that."

"Which way did the gunfighter go?" Hays asked.

"I don't know," Benson said, shaking his head. "I just come straight along the trail to catch up. I figured you would want to know."

Benson was now aware that he should have just ridden on, like he had planned. Hays wasn't happy to hear about the woman or the gunfighter. He was worried about himself and what was going to happen. He was even thinking that there was a plot against him somehow.

This made Benson wonder about Carson Hays and what was going through his head. Was he going to shoot everybody he suddenly got worried about? Benson knew the others were wondering the same thing. It wasn't safe to be a part of the Hays Gang any longer. It was, in fact, very dangerous.

"I'm still not real sure about you," Hays then told Benson. "But we'll wait until later to settle that."

18

THE SUN WAS JUST RISING when Lassiter rode up Arrow Creek. He used the same trail he and Lorna had used before to reach Lanna's cabin. This time he wasn't cautious, but rode straight in.

He reached the cabin, and Lanna met him with her rifle in the crook of her arm.

"I surely didn't expect to see you back here again. Where's Lorna?"

"I lost her," Lassiter explained. "I was hoping she'd come here, but I guess she went on to Rocky Point like she said she was going to do."

Lanna frowned. "Rocky Point? I thought she was headed back to Kansas City."

"Just before we came here looking for you," Lassiter explained, "she took a fall from the mare she was riding. She banged her head again. Part of the Hays Gang was after us. After we found you, and she learned you didn't want to go back with her, she started acting funny, mentioning Rocky Point a lot. I think she's confused again and is looking for you like she did the first time."

"Haven't seen her back here," Lanna said. "When did she get away from you?"

"Last night. A bunch led by Carson Hays rousted us from sleep. I put her into hiding and led them off on a chase. When I got back, she was gone."

Lanna took a deep breath. "She's headed right into trouble, no doubt about that. If Carson's looking for me, and she's out on her own, there's no doubt he'll find her. Does he know I have a sister?"

Lassiter nodded. "He learned about the gunfight my friend and I had at Fort Benton with some of his men. A bartender told him all of it, including the fact that Lorna left with me to find you. Then I got the drop on one of his men last night and told him about Lorna. I let him go, and he went straight to Hays with the news."

Lanna shook her head. "I guess I knew it would come to something like this sooner or later. I didn't know it would be this complicated, but I realized that one day I would be meeting up with Carson again."

"You don't have to get involved," Lassiter told her. "I just came by in hopes Lorna had remembered Arrow Creek and rode up here. You aren't really part of this anymore."

"Of course I am," Lanna insisted. "First of all, Carson Hays is my husband. Sooner or later, I've got to put a stop to his madness. Secondly, and more importantly, Lorna is my flesh and blood. If for no other reason than that, I'm going to see this through to the end."

"Hays's quarrel now is really with me," Lassiter said. "No need to put yourself in danger."

"I've been in danger all my life," Lanna said quickly. "I'm used to it. If you'll wait for me a moment, I'll put a change of clothes in a bag. Then I'll catch my horse and be right with you.''

Ben Morris stopped his horse at the crest of a hill and waited for Darren Jackson to catch up. Jackson was frowning as he reined in his horse beside Morris's.

"You've got to do better than that, Darren," Morris chided him. "I'm crippled, and I can ride without all the fuss."

"I'm not used to this sort of thing, you know," Jackson protested. "I'm so sore I can hardly move." He got down from the saddle and groaned.

"Rocky Point is just ahead," Morris told him. "Why don't you hold off with stiffening up until we get you near a tub of hot water?"

"Are you sure they have such a thing down there?" Jackson asked. "It doesn't look like much more than a few log cabins to me."

"There's more down there than we've got up here," Morris pointed out. "Get back on your horse and let's go."

They found Rocky Point nearly deserted. The freight wagons had come and gone the day before, and there were no steamboats. The Fourth of July had been a notable exception to the general rule. Steamboats that stopped for any reason but curiosity were few and far between.

There were only a few cowhands in town, all of them drinking at the saloon. Morris limped in with Darren Jackson behind him. One of the men drinking at the bar took special note of Morris and Jackson, then turned back to his drinking.

Jackson looked around the inside of the saloon, shaking his head in disbelief. He had grown up in the big city. He once again went to look out into the street, as Morris ordered whiskey for both of them.

"I would never have believed towns like this existed," he told Morris, returning for his whiskey.

"This is how Kansas City started out," Morris told him, uncorking the bottle. "The very same way."

Jackson grunted. "You mean this place is going to rival Kansas City in time?"

"Never can tell," Morris said with a grin. "But I don't suppose you'd like to stick around to find out."

"Not on your life," Jackson said, downing his whiskey. He poured himself another. "As soon as I find Lorna, I'm getting out of here as fast as I can."

The interested cowhand turned again to look at Jackson and Morris. His eyes widened a bit, and he turned away again.

"You can bet on that," Morris agreed with Jackson. "As soon as our business is done, we're gone."

The bartender, overhearing the conversation, laughed. "That's why this is no Kansas City," he commented. "Everybody who stops here wants to get out as fast as they can."

Jackson then showed the bartender the same photograph Morris had been showing around. "I'm looking for a woman." He had his finger on Lorna.

The cowhand watched closely as the bartender nodded and motioned with his head. "She came in late last night and fell into a bed at the hotel. From what I hear, she hasn't moved since."

"Does anyone else know she's here?" Morris asked the bartender.

The bartender shrugged. "I never have seen her myself. I just heard about her. They say she don't know who she is."

Jackson thanked the bartender and turned with Morris for the door. The cowhand listening to the conversation moved to a window and watched.

Jackson and Morris went quickly up the short, dusty street and were soon talking to an old man who sat out front of the hotel smoking a thick, hand-rolled cigarette.

"Do you run this hotel?" Jackson asked urgently.

The old man squinted. "Who wants to know?"

Jackson pulled the photo. "I understand this woman came into town last night and she's lost, she doesn't know who she is."

The old man studied the picture. His eyes went to Jackson and the picture, back and forth.

"You her husband, or something?"

"Yes, I'm her husband. Is she still in the hotel?"

"Room number five," he said, spitting a wisp of tobacco that clung tenaciously to his lip. "But she's scared as a holed-up rabbit."

"Thanks for your help," Jackson said.

As they knocked on number five, Morris told Jackson that they had better be prepared to tie her up.

"There's really no need for that," Jackson said. "She'll know who I am."

There was no answer, and Jackson knocked again and again, calling for Lorna. Finally, Morris went back to the old man.

"We need to have you let us in," Morris told him.

"I'm not surprised," the old man said. "I couldn't rouse her earlier. But I didn't want to disturb her, so I didn't open the door. . . . You sure he's her husband?"

"You saw the picture," Morris said impatiently. "Hurry up, will you?"

The old man led the way back toward the room, fumbling in his pocket for keys, which he brought out and sorted leisurely in front of the door, where Jackson waited, his brow wrinkled with added impatience and worry. Finally, the old man jammed a key into the lock and turned the handle.

Lorna burst from the door, knocking the old man over. She rushed out into the light and began to run across the dusty street toward the river. Brush lay ahead of her, thick growths of trees and brush. If she could just reach the river and hide—

The interested cowhand from the saloon, a man named Jameson, saw Lorna running and went from the saloon directly to his horse. No one paid much attention as he casually rode out of town, looking back over his shoulder on occasion. After getting a ways out, he kicked his horse into a dead run.

Lorna was still running toward the river. Jackson yelled after her and began to give chase. Morris hobbled along behind, while the astonished old man picked himself up, brushed ashes and tobacco from his front, and stared after them.

Jackson finally caught Lorna just before she reached the trees. She went to the ground, yelling and kicking, as Jackson tried to calm her. Finally, with Morris's arrival and help, Darren Jackson got his wife calmed down.

"Lorna, you've got to know who I am," he said. He showed her the picture.

Lorna's breath caught in her throat. The picture. Once again her eyes flooded with tears. She remembered now who she was and why she was here. She remembered Lassiter.

"Is Mr. Lassiter with you?"

"No," Jackson said.

"Where is Lassiter?" Morris suddenly asked. "How'd you get here without him?"

"We ran into outlaws during the night," Lorna said, remembering the event. "He hid me in the brush along the river while he led them on a chase. I don't know, I got scared and rode off here. I was thinking I wanted to find Lanna. I was confused—I've been confused—a lot lately.''

Lorna told them the story of finding Lanna's cabin hidden deep in the badlands along Arrow Creek, and how Lanna had decided to stay there and not go to Kansas City. She noticed how her husband's face clouded with worry.

"I just need time," Lorna said. "Time and rest."

"Your sister's not interested in going back to Kansas City with us?" Jackson asked.

"I tried and tried to talk her into it, but she wouldn't," Lorna said. "She wants nothing to do with the big city. I guess I took it pretty hard. That was after I took another fall and hit my head. I hardly even remember talking to Lanna at all."

"And you haven't seen Lassiter since last night?" Morris said.

Lorna shook her head. "Not since he took off to lead the outlaws away from our camp."

"Do you suppose they killed him?" Jackson asked Morris.

Morris shook his head. "Not likely. Not at night, not on the horse he rides. There's not many horses can keep up with that stallion of his."

Jackson turned back to Lorna. "It doesn't matter now," he said. "I've found you and we can get started for Kansas City."

Lorna shook her head. "Oh, no. We can't leave yet. We can't leave without Lassiter."

"What are you talking about?" Jackson asked. "I've found you. I'll make sure Ben, here, gets his money to him."

"That's not what she's saying," Morris said to Jackson. "She's trying to tell you that Lassiter is the only reason that Lorna is still safe. We need him to help us keep it that way."

"Ben's right," Lorna said. "There's an outlaw named Carson Hays close by here somewhere. He'll find us if we leave without Lassiter. We won't have a chance."

Jackson looked up at Morris. "Is this the case? Do we need this Lassiter that badly for protection?"

"You bet we do," Morris agreed. "I told you about Carson Hays and his gang. Lorna's already met some of them. Take her word for it, we need Lassiter to leave this country."

"Please, Darren," Lorna begged. "You have to understand. These outlaws are killers."

"Well, where is this Lassiter?" Jackson asked. "He can't help us if he isn't here, and we can't wait forever."

"We'll wait as long as we have to," Morris said to Jackson. He turned to Lorna. "Did Lassiter have any idea where you might have ridden off to?"

"He knows I came back in this direction," Lorna said. "I kept telling him I wanted to find Lanna back here at Rocky Point. He'll be back here before long looking for me. I know that."

"What about the outlaws?" Jackson said. "What's to keep them from causing us trouble right here?"

"They could very well cause us trouble right here," Morris told him. "But they would certainly cause us a lot more trouble if they caught us out in the open somewhere."

"So what do we do now?" Jackson asked.

"It's my guess that both the outlaws and Lassiter will be headed this way, if they haven't shot it out already," Morris said. "In any case, we'd best hole up in the saloon and hope that Lassiter gets here first."

19

CARSON HAYS STOOD LOOKING at Jeff's grave. He and the others had been back less than an hour, and already Hays was beginning to wonder what was going on. Nothing was anywhere near the same as it had been when he left for Fort Benton.

Jeff was dead, and now Lonnie didn't even seem like his brother any longer. He watched Lonnie walk from the cabins up the hill toward him after having had a long talk with the men. It seemed they all wanted to quit the gang.

Hays was beside himself with anger. Somehow he had lost control over things, and it wouldn't do any good to just shoot everyone. He wouldn't have a gang left to steal horses.

Everything had changed forever. He still wasn't over the shock of learning about Jeff's death, and he was considering forgetting about Lanna for the time being. Now he would search for that gunfighter.

Though the gunfighter hadn't personally hanged Jeff, Carson Hays believed it wouldn't have happened if he hadn't been there. Will Carlson and the others must have gotten their courage from him.

Hays now wondered why he hadn't worked harder at getting him the night before. It hadn't seemed all that important at the time, but now it was uppermost in his mind.

Ater learning about his brother Jeff and the others who had fallen to the gunfighter's guns, Carson Hays wasn't that impressed with the news that Lonnie gave him about wiping out Will Carlson and his stranglers. It no longer mattered that the roan was his, out grazing among the other horses.

It no longer mattered that his previous adversary, Will Carlson, would no longer be around to cause trouble. There would be no sweet revenge for Jeff until he got this stranger and put him down for good.

The devastating loss of his little brother was much more of a blow than Carson Hays wanted to admit. In Fort Benton, he had learned about losing men to this stranger and it had bothered him, but he hadn't given much thought to anything else like that happening. No one had ever stood up to his gang before.

He reflected again on how their business of moving horses had gone on without a hitch until this stranger had showed up. He gripped the shell casings on his vest and squeezed, almost tearing them off in places. He wanted to add one special casing to his collection. He would attach it where it stood out from all the others. He would do it real soon.

At first, he had listened to the whole story about what had happened during the Fourth of July celebration and had blamed Lonnie. But Lonnie had talked back to him, and Benson and the other men stood behind him. That had never happened before.

As Lonnie approached Jeff's grave and stood beside him, Carson Hays could see tension in his brother's face.

"What did the men say?" Carson asked.

"We've got to get those brands changed on them horses and get them moved," Lonnie said. "I agree with them. Someone else is going to find us before we can find another place to hide out."

"We don't need another place to hide out."

"Yes, we do," Lonnie argued. "Someone else is bound to find us again. We've got to move around."

"I don't care about any of that now," Carson Hays said angrily. "I'm going to get that gunfighter."

Lonnie could hold his anger in no longer. "What the hell is this?" he asked. "First it was Lanna, and now this gunfighter. When are we going to get back to work?"

"I'll say when we get back to work!"

"Wrong! We took a vote. I'm leading the bunch with you now. It ain't just what you say that goes no more. We have to both agree."

"What are you talking about?"

"You heard me. You ain't the only boss now. And if you don't like it, the men all agreed that I'd take over myself."

Carson Hays stared in disbelief.

"That's right," Lonnie continued. "We've got work to do, and you don't care. It won't do no good to brood any more over what happened to Jeff. It was Jeff's doing, plain and simple."

"You were supposed to look out for him," Carson Hays said through clenched teeth.

"That was Jeff's trouble all the time," Lonnie said. "He thought somebody, usually you, could get him out of all his problems. That's what caused him to die."

"But you were here with him," Carson said. "Why didn't you watch him?"

"I wasn't with him when he got himself in trouble," Lonnie pointed out. "I was here, watching the horses *you* didn't want to move right away. It was more important to run off to Fort Benton and leave us undermanned. So don't tell me who's to blame for all this."

Carson Hays glared at his brother. "You think you can just stand there and tell me you're changing the way this gang operates, whether I like it or not."

"That's what I'm telling you," Lonnie said firmly.

"Kin or not," Carson said flatly, "I'd have to kill a man who tried to do that to me."

"Anything happens to me," Lonnie was now pointing down the hill at the rest of the gang, each of them holding a rifle, "and you won't live, either. That's for all time. You'd best get used to it."

"You don't sound like any brother of mine," Carson said. "In fact you don't talk like any Hays I ever knew."

"I'm talking like a Hays who's going to start using his head," Lonnie said. "We ain't been using our heads."

"I know what to do," Carson said, wondering to himself why he was in a position where he was having to defend himself to his little brother.

"You don't know what to do, not when real trouble comes for the whole bunch of us," Lonnie said. "You've killed a lot of men and you're fast with a gun, but this stranger is different. And with Lanna, well, you've gone plumb crazy. You just ain't about to make things so hard for us any longer."

Carson Hays couldn't believe this was happening to him. He stood speechless, staring first at his brother, Lonnie, and then down at the men he used to lead, now all grouped together against him.

This would not do, Carson Hays was thinking. He was considering how he was going to have to kill them all, even Lonnie, when he turned his eyes toward the trail coming into the hideout. There was the sound of hoofbeats as a rider appeared, spurring his horse down toward the cabins. Jameson was riding at full speed.

Carson Hays, his mind in turmoil, descended the hill with Lonnie to see what had excited Jameson.

Jameson jumped down from his horse. "I just came from town. I seen two men chasing a woman that looked like the one who shot Jeff in the leg, the one who looks just like Lanna."

"Was that stranger one of them?" Carson Hays asked.

Jameson shook his head. "No. I never seen them before. I know what that stranger looks like. But that woman—it had to be her. She was wearing the same dress and all."

"I told you she'd come this way," Benson told Carson Hays. "What did I tell you?"

Carson Hays ignored him. "What about that stranger?" he asked Jameson. "Where's he at?"

Jameson shrugged. "I told you, I don't know."

Carson Hays's eyes grew wide and wild. No one could really tell what he was thinking, just that he was getting angrier and wanted someone to blame for it.

"There ain't no call to get mad at anybody here," Lonnie then spoke up. "You'd ought to just go and find that gunfighter, if you want to so bad. That's what you'd ought to do."

Hays looked at his brother. "What do you mean *I'd* ought to find that gunfighter. It was your brother he killed, too."

"I ain't going up against him, Carson," Lonnie announced. "And none of the others will, either. We all stand together on that. I told you up at the grave, things have changed. You do what we all decided on this, or leave the outfit."

Jameson's eyebrows raised. The other men then told him about their meeting and how they'd decided not to let Carson be the sole leader any longer. They wanted to get back to the business of stealing horses.

"I see you all have turned yellow-bellied on me," Carson Hays said to the group with contempt. "You don't want to get that stranger after all he's done to our bunch?"

"You're the only one who can shoot like him," Lonnie said, speaking for everyone. "We don't want no part of him no more. We've seen enough. Besides, we don't think he even wants to stay around this country."

"What are you talking about?" Hays asked.

"He'll take Lanna's twin sister and be gone soon," Lonnie explained. "That's what he come for in the first place. Jameson's been in town off and on, and he learned that. Besides, we can't move horses when we're spread out all over the country like this. We're going back to work. What are you going to do?"

Carson Hays glared at his brother. "Have it your way. I'll just leave." He turned and walked a few steps toward his horse.

At that point in time, Carson Hays didn't care whether he lived or died, though he knew well enough he wasn't going to die. He pulled his pistol as he turned back and fanned two bullets into Lonnie's midsection and emptied the gun on the rest of the gang, killing Jameson outright and wounding two more.

Benson and two others were left. Benson ran for his horse while the other two took cover in the cabins. Hays took his rifle from its scabbard on his horse's saddle and casually shot Benson from his horse.

He replaced the rifle and climbed on his horse, watching for any gunfire coming from the cabins. Cowards, all of them. He stared down at Lonnie's body a moment before he kicked his horse into a gallop toward Rocky Point.

Lassiter rode into Rocky Point with Lanna and dismounted at the hitching post in front of the saloon. Lassiter recognized Morris's horse right away, but there was a horse next to Morris's that he didn't know.

Ben Morris and Darren Jackson burst outside as Lassiter finished throwing the reins over the pole. Lorna was with them, looking tired but more herself than the day before. She must have gotten her memory back.

"I'm sorry, Mr. Lassiter," she said. "I was out of my head again."

"I'm glad you got here," Lassiter said. "How did you manage to escape Carson Hays?"

Lorna shook her head. "I guess you diverted them long enough for me to get away."

"We knew you'd make it sooner or later," Morris told Lassiter. He introduced Darren Jackson, who was staring at Lanna.

"They look a lot alike, don't they?" Lassiter said to Jackson.

"It's uncanny," Jackson said. "If they weren't dressed so differently, I wouldn't know which was which."

"Which brings me to an idea that I have," Lanna then said, taking the bag of clothes off her saddle. She handed the bag to Lorna. "Get into those, and we'll meet Carson Hays with Lassiter. What do you say?"

Lorna looked into the bag. "You want me to dress in your clothes, so we look identical?"

Lanna nodded. "That will give Carson something to think about while Mr. Lassiter talks to him about leaving the country."

Darren Jackson's face clouded with worry. "Do you really think that's a good idea?" he asked Lanna.

"Anything to get rid of him is a good idea," Lanna said. "You don't know the man, and I'll guarantee you, you don't want to."

"But what if there's shooting?" Jackson asked.

"We've worked that out, Mr. Jackson," Lassiter assured him. "Neither of the women will be in any danger, I can promise you that."

Jackson shrugged. He turned to Morris.

"I trust Lassiter," Morris said.

"Very well," Jackson said. "How is this thing going to happen then?"

Lassiter turned to a cloud of dust coming from just north of town, dust made by a single rider.

"What do you make of that, Lassiter?" Morris asked him.

"Something doesn't fit," Lassiter said.

It was soon apparent that Carson Hays was alone. He rode to the edge of town and stopped his horse. Lassiter considered that it could be a trick, but could see no more dust coming from any direction. Hays had to be alone.

"That don't look right," Ben Morris said. "Carson Hays all by himself?" He turned to Lassiter. "You didn't drop all the rest of them, did you?"

Lassiter smiled. "Not by a long shot. You take everyone into the saloon and I'll see what we're up against."

20

Lassiter waited in the street in front of the saloon while Carson Hays dismounted. Lassiter had faced gunmen with reputations every bit as widespread as the one Hays enjoyed, and he knew from experience that a lot of talk about a man means nothing. Hays might have faced a lot of men himself, but that didn't mean he couldn't be beaten.

Hays got down slowly from his horse, a man with a deadly purpose. He tried to impress Lassiter with his cool demeanor. He held the reins for a short time, then tied them to a hitching post in front of an abandoned blacksmith shop.

He began a slow walk toward Lassiter and stopped in the street. Lassiter noted the gun casings sewn into his vest. Hays had his chest stuck out, so Lassiter couldn't miss them.

"So you're the one who's causing so much trouble," Hays yelled out to Lassiter. "You started something that's about to get you killed, mister."

Lassiter tried not to smile openly. He knew right away

that Carson Hays had never walked toward a man who just stood calmly. Hays was bothered by this and it showed.

"Judging from what I see," Hays continued, trying to disturb Lassiter, "I can't figure why anybody would be afraid of you."

"Nobody has to be afraid of me," Lassiter said calmly. "So why are you afraid of me?"

Lassiter could see that he was bothering Hays even more. As Lassiter had guessed, Hays was a mindless killer. But he was intelligent and wasn't so dense that words didn't affect him. That was good. If he didn't respond to the words, there would be nothing to do but draw and hope for the best.

Hays measured his response. "I've never been afraid of anybody in my life. I thought you might be the first, but I was wrong. Except for the clothes, you ain't what I expected at all."

"What were you looking for, Hays?" Lassiter asked him, smiling confidently. He stood calmly, his hands at his sides. "What kind of man did you expect to find? Shiftless and arrogant, like you? Somebody lost? Somebody who can't tell when they've reached the end?"

Hays tried to control his anger. He smiled, but it did little good. He was soon going to be shaking with rage.

"I just figured I'd find somebody who'd impress me," he finally said. "You don't look like nothing to me."

"Is that why you came alone?" Lassiter asked him. "Did you think you'd find somebody who wouldn't impress you? Or have your men given up on you?"

Hays was silent. Lassiter could see him stiffen ever so slightly. The rage was coming on.

"I'll bet that's it," Lassiter continued. "I'll bet your men just didn't want to come. You're on your own now. Nobody wants anything to do with you."

"I don't need anybody," Hays said defensively. "I don't need anybody with me at all."

Lassiter continued to taunt him. "I'll bet you didn't have a choice. Otherwise, you'd have made them come along for support, wouldn't you? You'd have made them back you up."

Hays was glaring.

"I'll bet this is the first time you haven't had them with you when you faced a man down," Lassiter continued. "Am I right? You used to have a gang who'd stand behind you. Now you've got nothing."

Lassiter could see Hays was getting angry and frustrated with his insight. He could see that Hays was wondering how he knew so much about the gang and their problems. Lassiter decided he would tell Hays how he knew so much.

"Maybe you don't remember last night too well," Lassiter said to Hays. "You and some of your men chased me around until you gave up on me, then I got the drop on one of them. He was leading a horse with a dead man on it. Remember him?"

Hays could see Benson clearly in his mind, could see Benson riding hard through the night to tell him about the stranger and Lanna's twin sister. Now he could see Benson falling from his horse after he'd shot him.

"Your man told me a lot of things about you," Lassiter said. "You want to know what he said?" Lassiter stood silent and waited.

"What did he tell you?" Hays finally asked Lassiter.

"He told me he wanted no part of your gang any longer," Lassiter replied. "He told me you were going crazy. You know, he was right. You are crazy. Of course, he rode back to you anyway. But I'll bet it didn't do him any good. Where's he at now? And where's your brother, Lonnie?''

Hays was stiffening even more. The muscles in his jaw stood out.

''There must be some more secrets, Hays,'' Lassiter prodded. ''It sure seems odd to me that your gang wouldn't follow you here. That's mighty strange.''

''It doesn't matter what you think,'' Hays told him. ''You're the cause of these problems, and you're going to pay.''

''How much paying have you done already?'' Lassiter asked him. ''You lost a good woman, for one thing.''

''That's none of your concern!'' Hays blared.

Lorna and Lanna then came out of the saloon, both dressed in trail clothes. Lanna led Lorna and they walked together up from the saloon a ways, at an angle to Carson Hays.

''Everything's finished for you, Carson,'' Lorna told him. Lanna stood beside her sister and watched Hays's expression of surprise.

''When this is finished,'' Hays said, ''you're coming with me.''

Lanna then spoke up. ''No, I'm not. Nobody is going anywhere with you.''

Hays turned his eyes from Lorna to Lanna. ''Which one of you belongs to me?'' he asked.

''You don't own anything or anybody,'' Lorna said.

''She's right,'' Lanna said. ''Your best bet is to just ride out now, while you still can.''

Hays's face registered more frustration. It was obvious he couldn't tell them apart, and he was getting enraged at being made a fool of.

''It's goodbye,'' Lanna said. ''Take it from me, I'm the one who knows you.''

"Yes, Carson, it's goodbye," Lorna then mimicked.

The two sisters turned and walked back into the saloon. Lassiter stepped toward Hays.

"What's the matter, Hays?" Lassiter asked him. "Cat got your tongue?"

Hays stood motionless while Lassiter continued to walk slowly toward him.

"Face it, Hays," Lassiter continued, "you haven't got a chance now. You've had things your way for far too long. This is the end."

"Stop where you are!" Hays finally called out. "I'll draw on you. They'll bury you."

Lassiter ignored Hays and continued forward slowly, staring hard at the outlaw.

"Your days of thieving and killing are all done, Hays. You know it and so does everybody else."

"Nobody talks to me that way," Hays said through gritted teeth, his eyes blurred with hate.

Lassiter finally came to a stop less than five strides from Hays. "Why don't you just give yourself up, Hays?" he suggested. "Make it easy for everybody."

Lassiter was watching Hays closely, seeing how the anger and rage had overcome the outlaw, taking his reasoning. His muscles were tensing more and more as Lassiter stared him down.

Gradually, Carson Hays was losing more and more confidence in himself. He had never faced a man like Lassiter before, and there was no way out for him now.

"You look a little pale, Hays," Lassiter observed. "You want a glass of water? You want something to make you feel better? Too bad your mother isn't here for you."

Hays grabbed for his pistol. Lassiter was watching and moved his right hand like a flash for his Colt. Hays was incredibly fast and would have ordinarily been a lot smoother in his motion; but Lassiter had riddled his nerves and his sense of timing. Hays was no match for Lassiter.

Lassiter's Colt spit flame just as Hays's thumb pulled back the hammer on his pistol. One bullet, then another slammed into Hays's chest, sending him stumbling backward. His gun discharged into the dirt and he spun a half-circle before dropping to his knees.

Hays tried to cock and lift his pistol. He got the weapon partway up and tried to turn. He was too weak and growing steadily weaker. He managed to give Lassiter one last, long blank stare before falling forward in death.

Lassiter holstered his Colt and walked toward the outlaw. The saloon and hotel emptied. Lorna and Darren Jackson stood with Ben Morris, and Lanna stood next to Lassiter, staring down at the fallen outlaw.

"At least this will give some people around here a new start," Lassiter said.

Darrell Jackson put his arm around Lorna. "I believe this is a new start for a number of us," he said. "I know this has certainly made me reconsider what I think of as most important in life. I know without a doubt that it's my wife."

"I'll listen to you, Darren, and I'll do what it takes to recover from my fall," Lorna promised him.

A cowhand riding into town realized what had taken place and turned his horse to spread the news.

"I can't imagine what I ever saw in him," Lanna said. There was no emotion whatsoever in her voice. "I guess I was just a young girl wanting so much to be in love."

"You don't have to think about the past any longer," Lorna told her sister. "That's all over."

"There is still a lot of life ahead, isn't there?" Lanna said, smiling.

"I realize now that meeting you was something I had to

do,'' Lorna said, ''but that having you with me for the rest of our lives isn't necessary.'' She hugged Lanna. ''I can understand if you want to stay here, but I sure wish you'd come back with us.''

''I might get up the nerve to come down and visit some time,'' Lanna told Lorna. ''We'll see.''

Lanna watched as the bartender and the old man from the hotel dragged Carson Hays's body over to the saloon and propped him up against the log wall in a sitting position. His front was soaked with blood. The bartender pushed on the eyelids to try to open them fully, but they remained half-closed. It didn't matter. There would be a lot of folks who would travel a long way to get a look before he was put in the ground.

Lanna unhitched her horse and climbed into the saddle while the others watched the men preparing Carson Hays for viewing. Lassiter watched her while he untied the reins to his stallion.

''You watch yourself in this country,'' he told her. ''But I guess I don't have to say that.''

Lanna held her horse and reached down to shake Lassiter's hand. She held it firmly.

''You're like no other man I've ever met,'' she told him. ''I'm grateful that you brought my sister to see me, and I hope things go well for you. I can't see how things could get so bad you couldn't handle them, but I hope you are happy.''

''You take care of yourself,'' Lassiter said, tipping his hat.

Lanna then rode out of town into the badlands. She topped a rise in the distance and Lassiter noticed her turn and look back momentarily before riding down the other side of the slope.

Lassiter turned to shake Darren Jackson's hand.

"I don't know how to thank you enough for your help," Jackson told Lassiter. "You'll have a fine reward in the mail, I can promise you. Or better yet, I'd like to invite you down to Kansas City with us, if you'd care to spend some time down there."

Lassiter smiled, but declined the invitation. "I think I'll just spend a little time relaxing," he said, "like I'd planned to do all along. Thanks anyway."

Lorna came over and stood next to Lassiter, her eyes brimming with tears. "I don't know how to thank you for everything you've done," she said. "But be assured, if you ever need anything, Darren and I will be there for you."

Lassiter tipped his hat. "I'll remember that."

Ben Morris, who was standing beside him, cleared his throat. "I guess this was no vacation, but I'm glad to have a friend like you, somebody I can count on to see things through to the end. Friends like that are rare."

"Let's just say you owe me one," Lassiter said with a smile, shaking his hand firmly. "Are you headed back to Kansas City with the Jacksons?"

"I've got nothing to stay here for," Morris said. "Unless you've got an idea."

"Oh, no," Lassiter said, climbing on his stallion. "I'm fresh out of ideas. I need a rest."

"Where do you suppose we'll meet up again?" Morris asked Lassiter.

"Someplace without badlands and outlaws," Lassiter replied with a smile.

Lassiter turned his stallion and rode out of town into the badlands. Behind, the legacy of Carson Hays and his gang would be carried along the trails and into the saloons. By nightfall, all the cowhands in the area would be gathered, drinks in hand, around the body of Carson Hays.

Lassiter stopped to look back at the little town one last time. By the time it came alive, he would be out of the rough country. He hoped he would find a much softer and a much safer place to get some rest than the clay bottomlands he had come to know so well. He would leave them behind, but in a way he would miss them.